THE CHILDREN
OF THE KING

A Tale of Southern Italy

F. Marion Crawford

The Children of the King

F. Marion Crawford

© 1st World Library – Literary Society, 2006
PO Box 2211
Fairfield, IA 52556
www.1stworldlibrary.org
First Edition

LCCN: 2006930770

Softcover ISBN: 1-4218-2180-X
Hardcover ISBN: 1-4218-2080-3
eBook ISBN: 1-4218-2280-6

Purchase *"The Children of the King"*
as a traditional bound book at:
www.1stWorldLibrary.org/purchase.asp?ISBN=1-4218-2180-X

1st World Library Literary Society is a nonprofit
organization dedicated to promoting literacy by:

- Creating a free internet library accessible from any computer worldwide.
- Hosting writing competitions and offering book publishing scholarships.

Readers interested in supporting literacy
through sponsorship, donations or
membership please contact:
literacy@1stworldlibrary.org
Check us out at: www.1stworldlibrary.ORG
and start downloading free ebooks today.

The Children of the King
contributed by Tim, Ed & Rodney
in support of
1st World Library Literary Society

TO

THE MIDDY, THE LADDIE, THE MATE
AND THE MEN THE SKIPPER OF THE OLD
LEONE DEDICATES THIS STORY

CHAPTER I

Lay your course south-east half east from the Campanella. If the weather is what it should be in late summer you will have a fresh breeze on the starboard quarter from ten in the morning till four or five o'clock in the afternoon. Sail straight across the wide gulf of Salerno, and when you are over give the Licosa Point a wide berth, for the water is shallow and there are reefs along shore. Moreover there is no light on Licosa Point, and many a good ship has gone to pieces there in dark winter nights when the surf is rolling in. If the wind holds you may run on to Palinuro in a long day before the evening calm comes on, and the water turns oily and full of pink and green and violet streaks, and the sun settles down in the north-west. Then the big sails will hang like curtains from the long slanting yards, the slack sheets will dip down to the water, the rudder will knock softly against the stern-post as the gentle swell subsides. Then all is of a golden orange colour, then red as wine, then purple as grapes, then violet, then grey, then altogether shadowy as the stars come out - unless it chances that the moon is not yet full, and edges everything with silver on your left hand while the sunset dyes fade slowly to darkness upon your right.

Then the men forward will bestir themselves and presently a red glow rises and flickers and paints what it touches, with its own colours. The dry wood crackles and flares on the brick and mortar hearth, and the great kettle is put on. Presently the water boils - in go the long bundles of fine-drawn paste, and everybody collects forward to watch the important operation.

Stir it quickly at first. Let it boil till a bit of it is tender under the teeth. In with the coarse salt, and stir again. Up with kettle. Chill it with a quart of cold water from the keg. A hand with the colander and one with the wooden spoon while the milky boiling water is drained off. Garlic and oil, or tomato preserve? Whichever it is, be quick about it. And so to supper, with huge hard biscuit and stony cheese, and the full wine jug passed from mouth to mouth. To every man a fork and to every man his place within arm's length of the great basin - mottled green and white within, red brown and unglazed on the outside. But the man at the helm has an earthen plate, and the jug is passed aft to him from time to time.

Not that he has much to do as he lies there on his six-foot deck that narrows away so sharply to the stern. He has taken a hitch round the heavy tiller with the slack of the main sheet to keep it off the side of his head while he eats. There is no current, and there is not a breath of air. By and by, before midnight, you will smell the soft land breeze blowing in puffs out of every little bay and indentation. There is no order needed. The men silently brace the yards and change the sheets over. The small jib is already bent in place of the big one, for the night is dark and some of those smart puffs will soon be like little squalls. Full and by. Hug the land, for there are no more reefs before Scalea. If you do not get aground on what you can see in Calabria, you will not get aground at all, says the old proverb. Briskly over two or three miles to the next point, and the breeze is gone again. While she is still forging ahead out go the sweeps, six or eight of them, and the men throw themselves forward over the long slender loom, as they stand. Half an hour to row, or more perhaps. Down helm, as you meet the next puff, and the good felucca heels over a little. And so through the night, the breeze freshening before the rising sun to die away in the first hot morning hours, just as you are abreast of Camerota. L'Infresco Point is ahead, not three miles away. It is of no use to row, for the breeze will come up before long and save you the trouble. But the sea is white and motionless. Far in the offing a Sicilian schooner and a couple of clumsy "martinganes" - there is no proper English name for the craft - are lying becalmed, with hanging sails. The men on board the felucca watch them and the sea. There is a shadow on the white, hazy horizon, then a streak, then a broad dark blue band. The schooner braces her top-sail yard and gets her main sheet aft. The martinganes flatten in their jibs along their high steeving bowsprits and jib-booms. Shift your sheets, too, now, for the wind is coming. Past L'Infresco with its lovely harbour of refuge, lonely as a bay in a desert island, its silent shade and its ancient spring. The wind is south by west at first, but it will go round in an hour or two, and before noon you will make Scalea - stand out for the reef, the only one in Calabria - with a stern breeze. You have passed the most beautiful spot on the beautiful Italian coast, without seeing it. There, between the island of Dino and the cape lies San Nicola, with its grand deserted tower, its mighty cliffs, its deep, safe bay and its velvet sand. What matter? The wind is fair and you are for Calabria with twenty tons of macaroni from Amalfi. There is no time to be lost, either, for you will probably come home in ballast. Past Scalea, then, where tradition says that Judas Iscariot was born and bred and did his first murder. Right ahead is the sharp point of the Diamante, beyond that low shore where the cane brake grows to within fifty yards of the sea. Now you have run past the little cape, and are abreast of the beach. Down mainsail - down jib - down foresail. Let go the anchor while she forges, eight to nine lengths from the land, and let her swing round, stern to the sand. Clear away the dingy and launch her from amidships, and send a line ashore. Overboard with everything now, for beaching, capstan, chocks and all - the swell will wash them in. As the keel grates on the pebbles, the men jump into the water from the high stern and catch the drifting wood. Some plant the capstan, others pass the long hemp cable and reeve it through the fiddle block. A hand forward to slack out the cable as the heavy boat slowly creeps up out of the water. The men from other craft, already beached, lend a hand too and a score of stout fellows breast the long oars which serve for capstan bars. A little higher still. Now prop her securely and make all snug and ship-shape, and make fast the blade of an oar to one of the forward tholes, with the loom on the ground, for a ladder. You are safe in Calabria.

To-morrow at early dawn you must go into the hills, for you cannot sell a tenth of your cargo in the little village. Away you trudge on foot, across the rocky point, along the low flat beach by the cane brake, up the bed of the rivulet, where the wet green blades of the canes brush your face at every step. Shoes and stockings in hand you ford the shallow river, then, shod again, you begin the long ascent. You will need four good hours, or five, for you are not a landsman, your shoes hurt you, and you would rather reef top-sails - aye, and take the lee earing, too, in any gale and a score of times, than breast that mountain. It cannot be helped. It is a hard life, though there are lazy days in the summer months, when the wind will do your work for you. You must live, and earn your share; though they call you the master, neither boat nor cargo are yours, and you have to earn that share by harder work and with greater anxiety than the rest. But the world is green to-day. You remember a certain night last March - off Cape Orso in the gulf, when the wind they call the Punti di Salerno was raging down and you had a jib bent for a mainsail, and your foresail close reefed and were shipping more green water than you like to think of. Pitch dark, too, and the little lighthouse on the cape not doing its best, as it seemed. The long line of the Salerno lights on the weather bow. No getting there, either, and no getting anywhere else apparently. Then you tried your luck. Amalfi might not be blowing. It was no joke to go about just then, but you managed it somehow, because you had half a dozen brave fellows with you. As she came up she was near missing stays and you sang out to let go the main halyards. The yard came down close by your head and nearly killed you, but she paid-off all right and went over on the starboard tack. Just under the cape the water was smooth. Just beyond it the devil was loose with all his angels, for Amalfi was blowing its own little hurricane on its own account from another quarter. Nothing for it but to go about and try Salerno again. What could you do in an open felucca with the green water running over? You did your best. Five hours out of that pitch black night you beat up, first trying one harbour and then the other.

Amalfi gave in first, just as the waning moon rose, and you got under the breakwater at last.

You remember that last of your many narrow escapes to-day as you trudge up the stony mule-track through the green valleys, and it strikes you that after all it is easier to walk from Diamante all the way to Verbicaro, than to face a March storm in the gulf of Salerno in an open boat on a dark night. Up you go, past that strange ruin of the great Norman-Saracen castle standing alone on the steep little hill which rises out of the middle of the valley, commanding the roads on the right and the left. You have heard of the Saracens but not of the Normans. What kind of people lived there amongst those bristling ivy-grown towers? Thieves of course. Were they not Saracens and therefore Turks, according to your ethnology, and therefore brigands? It is odd that the government should have allowed them to build a castle just there. Perhaps they were stronger than the government. You have never heard of Count Roger, either, though you know the story of Judas Iscariot by heart as you have heard it told many a time in Scalea. Up you go, leaving the castle behind you, up to that square house they call the tower on the brow of the hill. It is a lonely road, a mere sheep track over the heights. You are over it at last, and that is Verbicaro, over there on the other side of the great valley, perched against the mountain side, a rough, grey mass of red-roofed houses cropping up like red-tipped rocks out of a vast, sloping vineyard. And now there are people on the road, slender, barefooted, brown women in dark wine-coloured woollen skirts and scarlet cloth bodices much the worse for wear, treading lightly under half-a-quintal weight of grapes; well-to-do peasant men - galantuomini, they are all called in Calabria - driving laden mules before them, their dark blue jackets flung upon one shoulder, their white stockings remarkably white, their short home-spun breeches far from ragged, as a rule, but their queer little pointed hats mostly colourless and weather-beaten. Boys and girls, too, meet you and stare at you, or overtake you at a great pace and almost run past you, with an enquiring backward glance, each carrying something - mostly grapes or figs. Out at last, by the little chapel, upon what is the beginning of an inland carriage road - in a land where even the one-wheeled wheelbarrow has never been seen. The grass grows thick among the broken stones, and men and beasts have made a narrow beaten track along the extreme outside edge of the precipice. The new bridge which was standing in all its spick and span newness when you came last year, is a ruin now, washed away by the spring freshets. A glance tells you that the massive-looking piers were hollow, built of one thickness of stone, shell-fashion, and filled with plain earth. Somebody must have cheated. Nothing new in that. They are all thieves nowadays, seeking to eat, as you say in your dialect, with a strict simplicity which leaves nothing to the imagination. At all events this bridge was a fraud, and the peasants clamber down a steep footpath they have made through its ruins, and up the other side.

And now you are in the town. The streets are paved, but Verbicaro is not Naples, not Salerno, not even Amalfi. The pavement is of the roughest cobble stones, and the pigs are the scavengers. Pigs everywhere, in the streets, in the houses, at the windows, on the steps of the church in the market-place, to right and left, before you and behind you - like the guns at Balaclava. You never heard of the Six Hundred, though your father was boatswain of a Palermo grain bark and lay three months in the harbour of Sebastapol during the fighting.

Pigs everywhere, black, grunting and happy. Red-skirted, scarlet-bodiced women everywhere, too, all moving and carrying something. Galantuomini loafing at most of the corners, smoking clay pipes with cane stems, and the great Jew shopkeeper's nose just visible from a distance as he stands in the door of his dingy den. Dirtier and dirtier grow the cobble stones as you go on. Brighter and brighter the huge bunches of red peppers fastened by every window, thicker and thicker on the upper walls and shaky balconies the black melons and yellowish grey cantelopes hung up to keep in the high fresh air, each slung in a hitch of yarn to a nail of its own.

Here and there some one greets you. What have you to sell?

Will you take a cargo of pears? Good this year, like all the fruit. The figs and grapes will not be dry for another month. They nod and move on, as you pass by them. Verbicaro is a commercial centre, in spite of the pigs. A tall, thin priest meets you, with a long black cigar in his mouth. When he catches your eye he takes it from between his teeth and knocks the ash off, seeing that you are a stranger. Perhaps it is not very clerical to smoke in the streets. But who cares? This is Verbicaro - and besides, it is not a pipe. Monks smoke pipes. Priests smoke cigars.

One more turn down a narrow lane - darkest and dirtiest of all the lanes, the cobble stones only showing here and there above the universal black puddle. Yet the air is not foul and many a broad street by the Basso Porto in Naples smells far worse. The keen high atmosphere of the Calabrian mountains is a mighty purifier of nastiness, and perhaps the pig is not to be despised after all, as sanitary engineer, scavenger and street sweeper.

This is Don Pietro Casale's house, the last on the right, with the steep staircase running up outside the building to the second story. And the staircase has an iron railing, and so narrows the lane that a broad shouldered man can just go by to the cabbage garden beyond without turning sideways. On the landing at the top, outside the closed door and waiting for visitors, sits the pig - a pig larger, better fed and by one shade of filthiness cleaner than other pigs. Don Pietro Casale has been seen to sweep his pig with a broken willow broom, after it has rained.

"Do you take him for a Christian?" asked his neighbour, in amazement, on the occasion.

"No," answered Don Pietro gravely. "He is certainly not a Christian. But why should he spoil the tablecloth with his muddy hog's back when my guests are at their meals? He is always running under the table for the scraps."

"And what are women for, except to wash tablecloths?"

inquired the neighbour contemptuously.

But he got no answer. Few people ever get more than one from Don Pietro Casale, whose eldest son is doing well at Buenos Ayres, and in whose house the postmaster takes his meals now that he is a widower.

For Don Pietro and his wife Donna Concetta sell their own wine and keep a cook-shop, besides a guest-room with a garret above it, and two beds, with an old-fashioned store of good linen in old-fashioned iron-bound chests. At the time of the fair they can put up a dozen or fourteen guests. People say indeed that the place is not so well managed, nor the cooking so good since poor Carmela died, the widow of Ruggiero dei Figli del Re - Roger of the Children of the King.

For this is the place where the Children of the King lived and died for many generations, and this house of Don Pietro Casale was theirs, and the one on the other side of the cabbage garden, a smaller and poorer one, in which Carmela died. The garden itself was once theirs, and the vineyard beyond, and the olive grove beyond that, and much good land in the valley. For they were galantuomini, and even thought themselves something better, and sometimes, when the wine was new, they talked of noble blood and said that their first ancestor had indeed been a son of a king who had given him all Verbicaro for his own. True it is, at least, that they had no other name. Through generation after generation they were christened Ruggiero, Guglielmo, and Sebastiano "of the Children of the King." Thus they had anciently appeared in the ill-kept parish registers, and thus was Ruggiero inscribed for the conscription under the new law.

And now, as you know, gaunt, weather-beaten Luigione, licensed master in the coast trade and just now captain of the Sorrentine felucca Giovannina, from Amalfi to Diamante with macaroni, there are no more of the Children of the King in old Verbicaro, and their goods have fallen into divers hands, but chiefly into those very grasping and close-holding ones of Don

Pietro Casale and his wife. But they are not all dead by any means, as you know also and you have even lately seen and talked with one of the fair-haired fellows, who bears the name.

For the Children of the King have almost always had yellow hair and blue eyes, though they have more than once taken to themselves black-browed, brown-skinned Calabrian girls as wives. And this makes one, who knows something more about your country than you do, Luigione - though in a less practical way I confess - this makes one think that they may be the modern descendants of some Norman knightling who took Verbicaro for himself one morning in the old days, and kept it; or perhaps even the far-off progeny of one of those bright-eyed, golden-locked Goths who made slaves of the degenerate Latins some thirteen centuries ago or more, and treated their serfs indeed more like cattle than slaves until almost the last of them were driven into the sea with their King Teias by Narses. But a few were left in the southern fastnesses and in the Samnite hills, and northward through the Apennines, scattered here and there where they had been able to hold their own; and some, it is said, forgot Theodoric and Witiges and Totila and Teias, and took service in the Imperial Guard at Constantinople, as Harold of Norway and some of our own hard-fisted sailor fathers did in later years.

Be that as it may - and no one knows how it was - the Children of the King have yellow hair and blue eyes to this present time, and no one would take them for Calabrians, nor for Sicilians, still less for monkey-limbed, hang-dog mouthed, lying, lubberly Neapolitans who can neither hand, reef nor steer, nor tell you the difference between a bowline and a buntling, though you may show them a dozen times, nor indeed can do anything but steal and blaspheme and be the foulest, filthiest crew that Captain Satan ever shipped for the Long Voyage. Not fit to slush down the mast of a collier, the best of them.

It must be a dozen years since Carmela died in that little house beyond the cabbage garden. It was a glorious night in

September - a strange night in some ways, and not like other nights one remembers, for the full moon had risen over the hills to the left, filling the world with a transparent vapour of silver, so clear and so bright that the very light seemed good to breathe as it is good to drink crystal water from a spring. Verbicaro was all asleep behind Don Pietro Casale's house, and in front, from the terrace before the guest-room, one could see the great valley far below beyond the cabbages, deep and mysterious, with silver-dashed shadows and sudden blacknesses, and bright points of white where the moon's rays fell upon a solitary hut. And on the other side of the valley, above Grisolia, a great round-topped mountain and on the top of the mountain an enormous globe of cloud, full of lightning that flashed unceasingly, so that the cloud was at one instant like a ball of silver in the moonlight, and at the next like a ball of fire in darkness. Not a breath stirred the air, and the strange thunderstorm flashed out its life through the long hours, stationary and alone at its vast height.

In the great silence two sounds broke the stillness from time to time; the deep satisfied grunt of a pig turning his fattest side to the cobble stones as he slept - and the long, low wail of a woman dying in great pain.

The little room was very dark. A single wick burned in the boat-shaped cup of the tall earthenware lamp, and there was little oil left in the small receptacle. On the high trestle bed, upon the thinnest of straw mattresses, decently covered with a coarse brown blanket, lay a pale woman, emaciated to a degree hardly credible. A clean white handkerchief was bound round her brow and covered her head, only a scanty lock or two of fair hair escaping at the side of her face. The features were calm and resigned, but when the pain of the death agony seized upon her the thin lips parted and deep lines of suffering appeared about the mouth; She seemed to struggle as best she could, but the low, quavering cry would not be stifled - lower and more trembling each time it was renewed.

An old barefooted friar with a kindly eye and a flowing grey

F. Marion Crawford

beard stood beside her. He had done what he could to comfort her and was going away. But she feebly begged him to stay a little longer. In an interval, while she had no pain, she spoke to her boys.

"Ruggiero - Sebastiano - dear sons - you could not save me, and I am going. God bless you. Our Lady help you - remember - you are Children of the King - remember - ah."

She sighed heavily and her jaw fell as another sort of pallor spread suddenly over her face. Poor Carmela was dead at last, after weeks of sickness, worked to death, as the neighbours said, by Pietro Casale and his wife Concetta.

She left those two boys, lean, poorly clad lads of ten and twelve years, yellow haired and blue eyed, with big bones and hunger-pinched faces. They could just remember seeing their father brought home dead with a knife wound in his breast six years earlier. Now they took hands as they looked at their dead mother with a sort of wondering gaze. There were no tears, no cries of despair - least of all did they show any fear.

Old Padre Michele made them kneel down, still hand in hand, while he recited prayers for the dead. The boys knew some of the responses, learned by ear with small regard for Latinity, though they understood what they were saying. When the monk got up they rose also and looked again at the poor dead face.

"You have no relations, my children," said the old man.

"We are alone," answered the elder boy in a quiet, clear voice. "But I will take care of Sebastiano."

"And I will help Ruggiero," said the younger in much the same tone.

"You are hungry?"

"Always," answered both together, without hesitation.

Padre Michele would have smiled, but the hungry faces and the mournful tone told him how true the spoken word must be. He fumbled in the pockets in the breast of his gown, and presently produced a few shady-looking red and white sugar sweetmeats, bullet-like in shape and hardness.

"It is all I have now, my children," said the old man. "I picked them up yesterday at a wedding, to give them to a poor little girl who was ill. But she was dead when I got there, so you may have them."

The lads took the stuff thankfully and crunched the stony balls with white, wolfish teeth.

With Padre Michele's help they got an old woman from amongst the neighbours to rouse herself and do what was necessary. When all was over she took the brown blanket as payment without asking for it, smuggling it out of the mean room under her great black handkerchief. But it was day then, and Don Pietro Casale was wide awake. He stopped her in the narrow part of the lane at the foot of his own staircase, and forcibly undid the bundle, to the old woman's inexpressible discomfiture. He said nothing, as he took it from her and carried it away, but his thin grey lips smiled quietly. The old woman shook her fist at him behind his back and cursed his dead under her breath. From Rome to Palermo, swear at a man if you please, call him by bad names, and he will laugh at you. But curse his dead relations or their souls, and you had better keep beyond the reach of his knife, or of his hands if he have no weapon. So the old woman was careful that Pietro Casale should not hear her.

"Managgia l'anima di chi t' e morto!" she muttered, as she hobbled away.

Everything in the room where Carmela died belonged to Don Pietro, and he took everything. He found the two boys standing together, looking across the fence of the cabbage garden down at the distant valley and over at the height opposite, beyond which the sea was hidden.

"Eh! You good-for-nothings!" he called out to them. "Is nothing done to-day because the mother is dead? No bread to-night, then - you know that."

"We will not work for you any more," answered Ruggiero, the elder, as both turned round.

Don Pietro went up to them. He had a short stout stick in his hand, tough and black with age, and he lifted it as though to drive them to work. They waited quietly till it should please him to come to close quarters, which he did without delay. I have said that he was a man of few words. But the Children of the King were not like Calabrian boys, children though they were. Their wolfish teeth were very white as they waited for him with parted lips, and there was an odd blue light in their eyes which is not often seen south of Goth-land.

They were but twelve and ten years old, but they could fight already, in their small way, and had tried it many a time with shepherd lads on the hill-side. But Don Pietro despised children and aimed a blow at Ruggiero's right shoulder. The blow did not take effect, but a moment had not passed before the old peasant lay sprawling on his back with both the boys on top of him.

"You cannot hurt the mother now," said Ruggiero. "Hit him as I do, Bastianello!"

And the four bony boyish fists fell in a storm of savage blows upon Don Pietro Casale's leathern face and eyes and head and thin grey lips.

"That is for the mother," said Ruggiero. "Another fifty a-piece for ourselves."

The wiry old peasant struggled desperately, and at last threw himself free of them and staggered to his feet.

"Quick, Bastianello!" shouted Ruggiero.

In the twinkling of an eye they were over the fence and running at full speed for the valley. Don Pietro bruised, dazed and half-blinded, struggled after them, crashing through hedges and stumbling into ditches while he shouted for help in his pursuit. But his heavy shoes hampered him, and at best he was no match for them in speed. His face was covered with purple blotches and his eyelids were swelling at a terrible rate. Out of breath and utterly worn out he stood still and steadied himself against a crooked olive-tree. He could no longer hear even the footsteps of the lads before him.

They were beyond his reach now. The last of the Children of the King had left Verbicaro, where their fathers had lived and died since darker ages than Calabrian history has accurately recorded.

CHAPTER II

"We shall never see him again," said Ruggiero, stopping at last and looking back over the stone wall he had just cleared.

Sebastiano listened intently. He was not tall enough to see over, but his ears were sharp.

"I do not hear him any more," he answered. "I hurt my hands on his nose," he added, thoughtfully, as he glanced at his bruised knuckles.

"So did I," returned his brother. "He will remember us. Come along - it is far to Scalea."

"To Scalea? Are we going to Scalea?"

"Eh! If not, where? And where else can we eat? Don Antonino will give us a piece of bread."

"There are figs here," suggested Sebastiano, looking up into the trees around them.

"It has not rained yet, and if you eat figs from the tree before it has rained you will have pain. But if we are very hungry we will eat them, all the same."

Little Sebastiano yielded rather reluctantly before his brother's superior wisdom. Besides, Padre Michele had given them a little cold bean porridge at the monastery early in the morning.

So they went on their way cautiously, and looking about them at every step now that there was no more need of haste. For they had got amongst the vineyards and orchards where they had no business, and if the peasants saw them, the stones would begin to fly. They knew their way about, however, and reached an open footpath without any adventure, so that in half an hour they were on the mule track to Scalea. They walked much faster than a grown peasant would have done, and they knew the road. Instead of turning to the left after going down the hill beyond the tower, they took the right hand path to the Scalea river, and as it had not rained they got across without getting very wet. But that road is not so good as the one to Diamante, because the river is sometimes swollen, and people with laden mules have to wait even as much as three days before they can try the ford, and moreover there is bad air there, which brings fever.

At last they struck the long beach and began to trudge through the sand.

"And what shall we do to-morrow?" asked Sebastiano.

Ruggiero was whistling loudly to show his younger brother that he was not tired nor afraid of anything. At the question he stopped suddenly, and faced the blazing blue sea.

"We can go to America," he said, after a moment's reflection.

Little Sebastiano did not seem at all surprised by the proposition, but he remained in deep thought for some moments, stamping up a little hillock of sand between his bare feet.

"We are not old enough to be married yet," he remarked at last.

"That is true," admitted Ruggiero, reluctantly.

Possibly, the close connection between going to America and

being married may not be apparent to the poor untutored foreign mind. It would certainly not have been understood a hundred miles north of Sebastiano's heap of sand. And yet it is very simple. In Calabria any strong young fellow with a decently good character can find a wife with a small dowry, though he be ever so penniless. Generally within a week, and always within a fortnight, he emigrates alone, taking all his wife's money with him and leaving her to work for her own living with her parents. He goes to Buenos Ayres or Monte Video. If, at the end of four, five or six years he has managed to increase the money so as to yield a small income, and if his wife behaves herself during his absence, he comes home again and buys a piece of land and builds a house. His friends do not fail to inform him of his wife's conduct, and he holds her dowry as a guarantee of her fidelity. But if he fails to enrich himself, or if she is unfaithful to him, he never comes back at all. It is thus clear that a penniless young man cannot go to America until he is married.

"That is very true," Ruggiero repeated.

"And we must eat," said Sebastiano, who knew by experience the truth of what he said.

"And we are always hungry. It is very strange. I am hungry now, and yet we had the beans only this morning. It is true that the plate was not full, and there were two of us. I wish we were like the son of Antonio, who never eats. I heard his mother telling the chemist so last winter."

"He is dead," said Sebastiano. "Health to us!" he added, according to custom.

"Health to us!" repeated Euggiero. "Perhaps he died because he did not eat. Who knows? I should, I am sure. Is he dead? I did not know. Come along! If Don Antonino is not away we shall get some bread."

So they trudged on through the sand. It was still very hot on the yellowish white beach, under the great southern sun in September, but the Children of the King had been used to bearing worse hardships than heat, or cold either, and the thought of the big brown loaves in Don Antonino's wine-shop was very cheering.

At last they reached the foot of the terraced village that rises with its tiers of white and brown houses from the shore to the top of the hill. Not so big nor so prosperous a place as Verbicaro, but much bigger and richer than Diamante. There are always a good many fishing boats hauled up on the beach, but you will not often see a cargo boat excepting in the autumn. Don Antonino keeps the cook-shop and the wine cellar in the little house facing the sea, before you turn to the right to go up into the village. He is an old sailor and an honest fellow, and comes from Massa, which is near Sorrento.

A vast old man he is, with keen, quiet grey eyes under heavy lids that droop and slant outward like the lifts of a yard. He is thickset, heavy, bulky in the girth, flat-footed, iron-handed, slow to move. He has a white beard like a friar, and wears a worsted cap. His skin, having lost at last the tan of thirty years, is like the rough side of light brown sole leather - a sort of yellowish, grey, dead-leaf colour. He is very deaf and therefore generally very silent. He has been boatswain on board of many a good ship and there are few ports from Batum to San Francisco where he has not cast anchor.

The boys saw him from a long way off, and their courage rose. He often came to Verbicaro to buy wine and had known their father, and knew them. He would certainly give them a piece of bread. As he saw them coming his quiet eyes watched them, and followed them as they came up the beach. But he did not turn his head, nor move hand or foot, even when they were close to him. He looked so solid and determined to stand still where he was, in the door of his shop, that you might have taken him for an enormous lay figure of a man, made of carved oak and dressed up for a sign to his own business. The two lads touched their ragged woollen caps and stood looking at him, wondering whether he would ever move. At last his grey eyes twinkled.

"Have you never seen a Christian before?" he inquired in a deep gruff voice.

He did not seem to be in a good humour. The boys drew back somewhat in awe, and sat down to rest on the stones by the wall. Still Antonino's eyes followed them, though he did not move. Sebastiano looked up at him uneasily from time to time, but Ruggiero gazed steadily at the sea with the affectation of proud indifference to scrutiny, which is becoming in a boy of twelve years. At last the old man stirred, turned slowly as on a pivot and went into the shop.

"Is it not better to speak to him?" asked Sebastiano of his brother in a whisper.

"No. He is deaf. If he did not understand us he would be angry and would give us no bread."

Presently Don Antonino came out again. He held half a loaf and a big slab of goat's-milk cheese between his huge thumb and finger. He paused exactly on the spot where he had stood so long, and seemed about to become absorbed in the contemplation of the empty fishing boats lying in the sun. Sebastiano watched him with hungry eyes, but Ruggiero again stared at the sea. After several minutes the old boatswain got under way again and came to them, holding out the food to them both.

"Eat," he said laconically.

They both jumped up and thanked him, and pulled at their ragged caps before they took the bread and cheese from his hand. He nodded gravely, which was his way of explaining that he could not hear but that it was all right, and then he watched them as they set to work.

"Like wolves," he said solemnly, as he looked on.

The place was quite deserted at that hour. Only now and then a woman passed, with an earthen jar of water on her head and her little tin bucket and rope in her hand. The public well is not fifty yards from Antonino's house, up the brook and on the left of it. The breeze was dying away and it was very hot, though the sun was already behind the high rocks of the cape.

"Where are the beasts?" asked Don Antonino, as the boys swallowed their last mouthful.

Ruggiero threw his head back and stuck out his chin, which signifies negation in the south. He knew it was of little use to speak unless he could get near the old man's ear and shout.

"And what are you doing here?" asked the latter.

Speech was now unavoidable. Ruggiero stood on tiptoe and the old man bent over sideways, much as a heavily laden Dutch galliot heels to a stiff breeze.

"The mother is dead!" bawled the boy in his high strong voice.

Oddly enough the tears came into his eyes for the first time, as he shouted at the deaf old man, and at the same moment little Sebastiano's lower lip trembled. Antonino shook his head in rough sympathy.

"We have also beaten Don Pietro Casale, and so we have run away," yelled the boy.

Antonino grunted thoughtfully and his grey eyes twinkled as he slowly righted himself and stood up again. Very deliberately he went into the shop again and presently came back with a big measure of weak wine and water.

"Drink," he said, holding out the jug.

Again the two boys pulled at their caps and each raised the jug respectfully toward the old man before drinking.

"To health," each said, and Antonino nodded gravely.

Then Ruggiero took the jug inside and rinsed it, as he knew it was his duty to do and set it on the table. When he came back he stood beside his brother, waiting for Don Antonino to speak. A long silence followed.

"Sleep," said the old man. "Afterwards we will talk."

He took his old place in the doorway and stared steadily out to sea. The boys lay down beside the house and having eaten and drunk their fill and walked a matter of fifteen miles, were sound asleep in three minutes.

At sunset Ruggiero sat up suddenly and rubbed his eyes. Don Antonino was no longer at the door, and the sound of several men's voices came from within, mingled with the occasional dull rattle of coarse glasses on wooden tables.

"O!" Ruggiero called softly to his brother. Then he added a syllable and called again, "O-e!" Little Sebastiano woke, sat up and looked about him, rubbing his eyes in his turn.

"What has happened?" he inquired, only half awake.

"By the grace of God we have eaten, we have drunk and we have slept," said Ruggiero by way of answer.

Both got up, shook themselves and stood with their hands in their pockets, looking at the sea. They were barefooted and barelegged, with torn breeches, coarse white shirts much patched about the shoulders, and ragged woollen caps. Presently they turned as by a common instinct and went and stood before the open door, peering in at the guests. Don Antonino was behind his black counter measuring wine. His wife was with him now and helping him, a cheerful, clean woman having a fair complexion, grey hair and round sharp eyes with red lids - a stranger in Calabria like her husband. She held the neck of a great pear-shaped demijohn, covered with straw, of which the lower part rested on the counter. Antonino held a quart jug to be filled while she lowered the mouth, and he poured the measure each time into a barrel through a black tin funnel. They both counted the measures in audible tones, checking each other as it were. The wine was very dark and strong and the smell filled the low room and came out through the door. Half-a-dozen men sat at the tables, mostly eating ship biscuit of their own and goat's-milk cheese which they bought with their wine. They were rough-looking fellows, generally in checked flannel shirts, and home-spun trousers. But they all wore boots or shoes, which are in the south a distinctive sign of a certain degree of prosperity. Most of them had black beards and smart woollen caps. They were men who got their living principally by the sea in one way or another, but none of them looked thorough seamen. They talked loud and with a certain air of boasting, they were rough, indeed, but not strongly built nor naturally easy in their movements as sailors are. Their eyes were restless and fiery, but the glance was neither keen nor direct. Altogether they contrasted oddly with Don Antonino, the old boatswain. This part of Calabria does not breed genuine sea folk.

Antonino took no notice of the boys as they stood outside the door, but went quietly on with his work, measuring quart after quart of wine and pouring it into the barrel.

"If it were a keg, I could carry it for him," said Ruggiero, "but I cannot lift a barrel yet."

"We could roll it, together," suggested Sebastiano thoughtfully.

Presently Don Antonino finished his job and bunged the barrel with a cork and a bit of old sailcloth. Then he looked up and stood still. The boys were not quite sure whether he was watching them or not, for it was already dusk. His wife lit a small German petroleum lamp and hung it in the middle of the room, and then went to the fireplace in the dark corner where something was cooking. One of the guests shouted to Antonino.

"There is a martingane at San Nicola," he bawled.

Antonino turned his head slowly to the speaker and waited for more.

"Bound east," continued the man. "From Majuri."

"What is wrong with her?" inquired the old host.

Boats going west, that is, towards Naples and Civita Vecchia often put in to the small natural harbours to wait for the night wind. Those going east never do except for some especial reason.

The man said nothing, but fixed his eyes on Antonino and slowly filled his pipe, evidently intending to convey some secret piece of information by the look and action. But the old sailor's stolid face did not betray the slightest intelligence. He turned away and deliberately took half-a-dozen salted sprats from a keg behind the counter and laid them in a dish preparatory to cleaning them for his own supper. The man who had spoken to him seemed annoyed, but only shrugged his shoulders impatiently and went on eating and drinking.

Antonino took a jug of water and went outside to wash his fish. The two boys offered to do it for him, but he shook his head. He did not speak until he had almost finished.

"We will fish to-night," he said at last, in a low voice, pouring a final rinsing of water into the dish. "Sleep in the sand under the third boat from the rocks. I will wake you when I am ready."

He looked from one to the other of the lads with a keen

glance, and then laid one huge finger against his lips. He drained the water from his dish and went in again.

"Come along," said Ruggiero softly. "Let us find the boat and get out of the way."

The craft was a small "gozzo," or fisherman's boat, not above a dozen or fourteen feet long, sharp and much alike at bow and stern, but with a high stem surmounted by a big ball of wood, very convenient for hanging nets upon. It was almost dark by this time, but the boys saw that she was black as compared with the other boats on both sides of her. She was quite empty and lay high and dry on three low chocks. Ruggiero lay down, getting as close to the keel as he could and Sebastiano followed his example. They lay head to head so that they could talk in a whisper.

"Why are we not to speak of his fishing?" asked the younger boy.

"Who knows? But if we do as he tells us he will give us more bread to-morrow."

"He is very good to us."

"Because we beat Don Pietro Casale. Don Pietro cheated him last year. I saw the cottonseed oil he mixed with the good, in that load we brought down."

"Perhaps the fishing is not for fish," suggested little Sebastiano, curling himself up and laying his head on the end of the chock.

They did not know what time it was when Don Antonino gently stirred them with his big foot. They sprang up wide awake and saw in the starlight that he had a pair of oars and a coil of rope in his hands.

"As I launch her, take the chocks from behind and put them in front," he said in a low voice.

F. Marion Crawford

Then he laid the oars softly in the bows and dropped the rope into the bottom, and began to push the boat slowly down to the sea. The boys did as he had told them to do, and in a few minutes the bows were in the rippling water. The old sailor took off his shoes and stockings and put them on board, and rolled up his trousers. Then with a strong push he sent her down over the pebbles and got upon the bows as she floated out. To look at his heavy form you would not have thought that he could move so lightly and quickly when he pleased. In a moment he was standing over the oars and backing to the beach again for the boys to get in. They stood above their knees in the warm water and handed him the chocks before they got on board. He nodded as though satisfied, but said nothing as he pulled away towards the rocky point. The lads sat silently in the stern, wondering whither he was taking them. He certainly had brought no fishing tackle with him. There was not even a torch and harpoon aboard for spearing the fish. He pulled rapidly and steadily as though he were going on an errand and were in a hurry, keeping close under the high rocks as soon as he was clear of the reefs at the cape. At last, nearly an hour after starting, the boys made out a great deserted tower just ahead. Then Antonino stopped pulling, unshipped his oars one after the other and muffled them just where the strap works on the thole-pin, by binding bits of sailcloth round them. He produced the canvas and the rope-yarn from his pockets, and the boys watched his quick, workmanlike movements without understanding what he was doing. When he began to pull again the oars made no noise against the tholes, and he dipped the blades gently into the water, as he pulled past the tower into the sheltered bay beyond.

Then a vessel loomed up suddenly under the great cliffs, and a moment later he was under her side, tapping softly against the planking. The boys held their breath and watched him. Presently a dark head appeared above the bulwarks and remained stationary for a while. Antonino stood up in his boat so as to lessen the distance and make himself more easily recognisable. Then a hand appeared beside the head and made a gesture, then dived down and came up again with the end of a rope, lowering it down into the boat. Antonino gave the line to Ruggiero and then stepped off upon the great hook on the martingane's side to which the chain links for beaching, got hold of the after shroud and swung himself on board.

Now it may be as well to say here what a martingane is. She is a good-sized, decked vessel, generally between five-and-twenty and a hundred tons, with good beam and full bows, narrow at the stern and rather high out of water unless very heavily laden. She has one stout mast, cross-trees, and a light topmast. She has an enormous yard, much longer than herself, on which is bent the high peaked mainsail. She carries a gaff-top-sail, fore-staysail, jib and flying-jib, and can rig out all sorts of light sails when she is before the wind. She is a good sea boat, but slow and clumsy, and needs a strong crew to handle her.

The two boys who sat in the fishing boat alongside the martingane on that dark night had no idea that all sea-going vessels were not called ships; but there was something mysteriously attractive to them in the black hull, the high tapering yard, and the shadowy rigging. They were certainly not imaginative boys, but they could not help wondering where the great dark thing had been and whither she might be going. They did not know what going to sea meant, nor what real deep-sea vessels were like, and they even fancied that this one might have been to America. But they understood well enough that they were to make no noise, and they kept their reflections to themselves, silently holding on to the end of the rope as they sat in their places.

They did not wait very long. In a few minutes Antonino and the other man came to the side, carrying an odd-looking black bundle, sewn up in what Ruggiero felt was oiled canvas as he steadied it down into the stern of the little boat, and neatly hitched round from end to end with spun-yarn, so as to be about the shape of an enormous sausage. The two men lowered it without much caution; it was heavy but rather limp. Then came another exactly like the first, which they also lowered into the boat, and a moment later Don Antonino came over the side as quickly and noiselessly as he had gone up, and shoved off quietly into the starlight.

Half an hour later he ran alongside of a narrow ledge of rock, apparently quite inaccessible from the land above, but running up along the cliff in such a way that, in case of danger from the sea, a man could get well out of reach of the breakers. He went ashore, taking the end of his own coil of rope with him. He made it fast in the dark shadow, and he must have known the place very well, for there was but one small hole running under a stone wedged in a cleft of the rock, through which he could pass the line. He got back into the boat.

"Get ashore, boys," he said, "and wait here. If you see a revenue boat, with coast guards in it, coming towards you as though the men wanted to speak to you, cast off the end of the rope and let it run into the sea. Then run up the ledge there, and climb the rock, the faster the better. There is a way up. But keep out of sight when it is day, by lying flat in the hollow there. If anybody else comes in a boat, and says nothing, but just takes the rope, do not hinder him. Let him take it, and he will take you too, and give you a couple of biscuits."

Don Antonino pushed off a little, letting the rope run out. Then he made his end of it fast to the two ends of the black bundles, and backing out as far as he could, he let them both down gently into the water, and pulled away, leaving the Children of the King alone on the ledge. He had managed to bring the rope down through the cleft, so that it could not easily be seen from the sea. The boys waited some time before either of them spoke, although the old fellow was deaf.

"Those things looked like dead men," said Sebastiano at last.

"But they are not," answered Ruggiero confidently. "Now I know why Don Antonino is so rich. He smuggles tobacco."

"If we could smuggle tobacco, too, it would be a fortune,"

remarked the younger boy. "He would give us bread every day, with cheese, and wine to drink."

"We shall see."

They sat a long time, waiting for something to happen, and then fell asleep, curling themselves up in the hollow as they had been told to do. At dawn they awoke and began to look out for the revenue boat. But she did not appear in sight. The hours were very long and it was very hot, and they had nothing to eat or drink. Then all at once they saw what seemed to them the most beautiful vision they could remember. A big felucca shot round the rocks, still under way from the breeze she had found in the little bay. Her full white sails still shivered in the sun, and the boys could see the blue light that passed up under her keel and was reflected upon her snow-white side as she ceased to move just in front of them.

A big man with a red beard and a white shirt stood at the helm and fixed his eyes on the point where the lads were hiding. He evidently saw them, for he nodded to a man near him and gave an order. In a moment the dingy was launched and a sailor came ashore. He jumped nimbly out, holding the painter of his boat in one hand, glanced at the boys, who stood up as soon as they saw that they were discovered, and cast off the end of the rope, keeping hold of it lest it should run. Then without paying any more attention to the boys, he went on board again taking the end with him.

"And we?" shouted Ruggiero after him, as he pulled away facing them.

"I do not know you," he answered.

"But we know you and Don Antonino," said Sebastiano, who was quick-witted.

"Wait a while," replied the sailor.

The man at the helm spoke to him while the others were hauling up the bundles out of the water and getting them on board. The dingy came rapidly back and the sailor sterned her to the rock for the boys to get in. In a few minutes they were over the side of the felucca.[1] They pulled at their ragged caps as they came up to the man at the helm, who proved to be the master.

[Footnote 1: A felucca is a two-masted boat of great length in proportion to her beam, and generally a very good sailer. She carries two very large lateen sails, uncommonly high at the peak, and one jib. She is sometimes quite open, sometimes half-decked, and sometimes fully decked, according to her size. She carries generally from ten to thirty tons of cargo, and is much used in the coasting trade, all the way from Civita Vecchia to the Diamante. The model of a first-rate felucca is very like that of a Viking's ship which was discovered not many years since in a mound in Norway.]

"What do you want?" he asked roughly, but he looked them over from head to foot, one at a time.

"The mother is dead," said Ruggiero, "and, moreover, we have beaten Don Pietro Casale and run away from Verbicaro, and we wish to be sailors."

"Verbicaro?" repeated the master. "Land folk, then. Have you ever been to sea?"

"No, but we are strong and can work."

"You may come with me to Sorrento. You will find work there. I am short-handed. I daresay you are worth a biscuit apiece."

He spoke in the roughest tone imaginable, and his black eyes - for he had black eyes and thick black hair in spite of his red beard - looked angry and fiery while he talked. Altogether you would have thought that he was in a very bad temper and not at all disposed to take a couple of starving lads on board out of charity. But he did not look at all such a man as those awkward, gaudily dressed, unsteady fellows the boys had seen in Antonino's shop on the previous night. He looked a seaman, every inch of him, and they instinctively felt that as he stood there at the helm he knew his business thoroughly and could manage his craft as coolly in a winter storm as on this flat September sea, when the men were getting the sweeps out because there was not a breath of wind to stir the sails.

"Go forward and pick beans for dinner," he said.

That was the first job given the Children of the King when they went to sea. For to sea they went and turned out seamen in due time, as good as the master who took them first, and perhaps a little better, though that is saying much.

And so I have told you who the Children of the King are and how they shipped as boys on board of a Sorrento felucca, being quite alone in the world, and now I will tell you of some things which happened to them afterwards, and not quite so long ago.

CHAPTER III

Ten years have passed since the ever-memorable day on which the Children of the King hurt their fists so badly in battering Don Pietro Casale's sharp nose. They are big, bony men, now, with strongly marked features, short yellow hair and fair beards. So far they are alike, and at first sight might be taken for twin brothers. But there is a marked difference between them in character, which shows itself in their faces. Ruggiero's eye is of a colder blue, is less mobile and of harder expression than Sebastiano's. His firm lips are generally tightly closed, and his square chin is bolder than his brother's. He is stronger, too, though not by very much, and though he is more silent and usually more equable, he has by far the worse temper of the two. At sea there is little to choose between them. Perhaps, on the whole, Sebastiano has always been the favourite amongst his companions, while Ruggiero has been thought the more responsible and possibly the more dangerous in a quarrel. Both, however, have acquired an extraordinarily good reputation as seamen, and also as boatmen on the pleasure craft of all sizes which sail the gulf of Naples during the summer season.

They have made several long voyages, too. They have been to New York and to Buenos Ayres and have seen many ports of Europe and America, and much weather of all sorts north and south of the Line. They have known what it is to be short of victuals five hundred miles from land with contrary winds; they have experienced the delights of a summer at New Orleans, waiting for a cargo and being eaten alive by mosquitoes; they have looked up, in January, at the ice-sheeted rigging, when boiling water froze upon the shrouds and ratlines, and the captain said that no man could lay out upon the top-sail yard, though the north-easter threatened to blow the sail out of the bolt-ropes - but Ruggiero got hold of the lee earing all the same and Sebastiano followed him, and the captain swore a strange oath in the Italo-American language, and went aloft himself to help light the sail out to windward, being still a young man and not liking to be beaten by a couple of beardless boys, as the two were then.[2] And they have seen many strange sights, sea-serpents not a few, and mermaids quite beyond the possibility of mistake, and men who can call the wind with four knots in a string and words unlearnable, and others who can alter the course of a waterspout by a secret spell, and a captain who made a floating beacon of junk soaked in petroleum in a tar-barrel and set it adrift and stood up on the quarter-deck calling on all the three hundred and sixty-five saints in the calendar out of the Neapolitan almanack he held - and got a breeze, too, for his pains, as Ruggiero adds with a quiet and somewhat incredulous smile when he has finished the yarn. All these things they have seen with their eyes, and many more which it is impossible to remember, but all equally astonishing though equally familiar to everybody who has been at sea ten years.

[Footnote 2: The writer knows of a Sorrentine captain, commanding a large bark who, when top-sails are reefed in his watch regularly takes the lee earing, which, as most landsmen need to be told, is the post of danger and honour.]

And now in mid-June they are at home again, since Sorrento is their home now, and they are inclined to take a turn with the pleasure boats by way of a change and engage themselves for the summer, Ruggiero with a gentleman from the north of Italy known as the Conte di San Miniato, and Sebastiano with a widowed Sicilian lady and her daughter, the Marchesa di Mola and the Signorina Beatrice Granmichele, generally, if incorrectly, spoken of as Donna Beatrice.

Now the Conte di San Miniato, though only a count, and reputed to be out at elbows, if not up to his ears in debt, is the sole surviving representative of a very great and ancient family in the north. But how the defunct Granmichele got his title of Marchese di Mola, no one knows precisely. Two things are certain, that his father never had a title at all, and that he himself made a large fortune in sulphur and paving stones, so that his only daughter is much of an heiress, and his elderly widow has a handsome income to spend as she pleases, owns in Palermo a fine palace - historical in other hands - is the possessor of a smartish yacht, a cutter of thirty tons or so, goes to Paris once and to Monte Carlo twice in every year, brings her own carriage to Sorrento in the summer, and lives altogether in a luxurious and highly correct manner.

She is a tall, thin woman of forty years or thereabouts, with high features, dark eyes, a pale olive complexion, black hair white at the temples, considerable taste in dress and an absolute contempt for physical exertion, mental occupation and punctuality.

Donna Beatrice, as they call her daughter, is a very pretty girl, aged nineteen or nearly, of greyhound build, so to say, by turns amazingly active and astonishingly indolent, capricious and decided in her caprices while they last, passionately fond of dancing, much inclined to amuse herself in her own way when her mother is not looking, and possessing a keen sense of prime and ultimate social ratios. She is unusually well educated, speaks three languages, knows that somehow North and South America are not exactly the same as the Northern and Southern States, has heard of Virgil and the Crusades, can play a waltz well, and possesses a very sweet little voice. She is undoubtedly pretty. Brown, on the whole, as to colouring - brown skin, liquid brown eyes, dark brown hair - a nose not regular but attractive, a mouth not small but expressive, eyebrows not finely pencilled, neither arched nor straight, but laid on as it were like the shadows in a clever charcoal drawing, with the finger, broad, effective, well turned, carelessly set in the right place by a hand that never makes mistakes.

It is the intention of the Marchesa di Mola to marry her daughter to the very noble and out-at-elbows Count of San Miniato before the summer is out. It is also the intention of the Count to marry Beatrice. It is Beatrice's intention to do nothing rashly, but to take as much time as she can get for making up her mind, and then to do exactly as she pleases. She perfectly appreciates her own position and knows that she can either marry a rich man of second-rate family, or a poor man of good blood, a younger son or a half ruined gentleman at large like San Miniato, and she hesitates. She is not quite sure of the value of money yet. It might be delightful to be even much richer than she is, because there are so many delightful things to be done in the world with money alone. But it might turn out to be equally agreeable to have a great name, to be somebody, to be a necessary part of society in short, because society does a number of agreeable things not wholly dependent upon cash for being pleasant, and indeed often largely dependent on credit.

San Miniato attracts her, and she does not deny the fact to herself. He is handsome, tall, fair, graceful and exceedingly well dressed. He was several years in a cavalry regiment and is reputed to have left the service in order to fight with a superior officer whom he disliked. In reality his straitened means may have had something to do with the step. At all events he scratched his major rather severely in the duel which took place, and has the reputation of a dangerous man with the sabre. It is said that the major's wife had something to do with the story. At present San Miniato is about thirty years of age. His only known vice is gambling, which is perhaps a chief source of income to him. Every one agrees in saying that he is the type of the honourable player, and that, if he wins on the whole, he owes his winnings to his superior coolness and skill. The fact that he gambles rather lends him an additional interest in the eyes of Beatrice, whose mother often plays and who would like to play herself.

Ruggiero, who is to be San Miniato's boatman this summer, is waiting outside the Count's door, until that idle gentleman wakes from his late sleep and calls him. The final agreement is yet to be made, and Ruggiero makes calculations upon his fingers as he sits on the box in the corridor. The Count wants a boat and three sailors by the month and if he is pleased, will keep them all the season. It became sufficiently clear to Ruggiero during the first interview that his future employer did not know the difference between a barge and a felucca, and he has had ocular demonstration that the Count cannot swim, for he has seen him in the water by the bathing-houses - a thorough landsman at all points. But there are two kinds of landsmen, those who are afraid, and those who are not, as Ruggiero well knows. The first kind are amusing and the sailors get more fun out of them than they know of; the second kind are dangerous and are apt to get more out of the sailor than they pay for, by bullying him and calling him a coward. But on the whole Ruggiero, being naturally very daring and singularly indifferent to life as a possession, hopes that San Miniato may turn out to be of the unreasonably reckless rather than of the tiresomely timid class, and is inclined to take his future master's courage for granted as he makes his calculations.

"I will take the Son of the Fool and the Cripple," he mutters decisively. "They are good men, and we can always have the Gull for a help when we need four."

A promising crew, by the names, say you of the North, who do not understand Southern ways. But in Sorrento and all down the coast, most seafaring men get nicknames under which their real and legal appellations disappear completely and are totally forgotten.

The Fool, whose son Ruggiero meant to engage, had earned his title in bygone days by dancing an English hornpipe for the amusement of his companions, the Gull owed his to the singular length and shape of his nose, and the Cripple had in early youth worn a pair of over-tight boots on Sundays, whereby he had limped sadly on the first day of every week, for nearly two years. So that the crew were all sound in mind and body in spite of their alarming names.

Ruggiero sat on the box and waited, meditating upon the probable occupations of gentlemen who habitually slept till ten o'clock in the morning and sometimes till twelve. From time to time he brushed an almost imperceptible particle of dust from his very smart blue cloth knees, and settled the in-turned collar of the perfectly new blue guernsey about his neck. It was new, and it scratched him disagreeably, but it was highly necessary to present a prosperous as well as a seamanlike appearance on such an important occasion. Nothing could have been more becoming to him than the dark close-fitting dress, showing as it did the immense breadth and depth of his chest, the clean-cut sinewy length of his limbs and the easy grace and strength of his whole carriage. His short straight fair hair was brushed, too, and his young yellow beard had been recently trimmed. Altogether a fine figure of a man as he sat there waiting.

Suddenly he was aware of a wonderful vision moving towards him down the broad corridor - a lovely dark face with liquid brown eyes, an exquisite figure clad in a well-fitted frock of white serge, a firm, smooth step that was not like any step he had ever heard. He rose quickly as she passed him, and the blood rushed to his face, up to the very roots of his hair.

Beatrice was too much of a woman not to see the effect she produced upon the poor sailor, and she nodded gracefully to him, in acknowledgment of his politeness in rising. As she did so she noticed on her part that the poor sailor was indeed a very remarkable specimen of a man, such as she had not often seen. She stopped and spoke to him.

"Are you the Count of San Miniato's boatman?" she asked in her sweet voice.

"Yes, Eccellenza," answered Ruggiero, still blushing violently

"Then he has engaged the boat? We want a boat, too - the

Marchesa di Mola - can you get us one?"

"There is my brother, Eccellenza."

"Is he a good sailor?"

"Better than I, Eccellenza."

Beatrice looked at the figure before her and smiled graciously.

"Send him to us at twelve o'clock," she said. "The Marchesa di Mola - do not forget."

"Yes, Eccellenza."

Ruggiero bowed respectfully, while Beatrice nodded again and passed on. Then he sat down again and waited, but his fingers no longer moved in calculations and his expression had changed. He sat still and stared in the direction of the corner beyond which the young girl had disappeared. He was conscious for the first time in his life that he possessed a heart, for the thing thumped and kicked violently under his blue guernsey, and he looked down at his broad chest with an odd expression of half-childish curiosity, fully expecting to see an outward and visible motion corresponding with the inward hammering. But he saw nothing. Solid ribs and solid muscles kept the obstreperous machine in its place.

"Malora!" he ejaculated to himself. "Worse than a cat in a sack!"

His hands, too, were quite cold, though it was a warm day. He noticed the fact as he passed his thumb for the hundredth time round his neck where the hard wool scratched him. To tell the truth he was somewhat alarmed. He had never been ill a day in his life, had never had as much as a headache, a bad cold or a touch of fever, and he began to think that something must be wrong. He said to himself that if such a thing happened to him again he would go to the chemist and ask for some medicine.

His strength was the chief of his few possessions, he thought, and it would be better to spend a franc at the chemist's than to let it be endangered. It was a serious matter. Suppose that the young lady, instead of speaking to him about a boat, had told him to pick up the box on which he was sitting - one of those big boxes these foreigners travel with - and to carry it upstairs, he would have cut a poor figure just at that moment, when his heart was thumping like a flat-fish in the bottom of a boat, and his hands were trembling with cold. If it chanced again, he would certainly go to Don Ciccio the chemist and buy a dose of something with a strong bad taste, the stronger and the worse flavoured the better, of course, as everyone knew. Very alarming, these symptoms!

Then he fell to thinking of the young lady herself, and she seemed to rise before him, just as he had seen her a few moments earlier. The signs of his new malady immediately grew worse again, and when it somehow struck him that he might serve her, and let Sebastiano be boatman to the Count, the pounding at his ribs became positively terrifying, and he jumped up and began to walk about. Just then the door opened suddenly and San Miniato put out his head.

"Are you the sailor who is to get me a boat?" he asked.

"Yes, Eccellenza," answered Ruggiero turning quickly, cap in hand. Strange to say, at the sound of the man's voice the alarming symptoms totally disappeared and Ruggiero was quite himself again.

He remembered also that he had been engaged for the Count, through the people of the hotel, on condition of approval, and that it would be contrary to boatman's honour to draw back. After all, too, women in a boat were always a nuisance at the best, and he liked the Count's face, and decided that he was not of the type of landsmen who are frightened. The interview did not last long.

"I shall wish to make excursions in all directions," said San

Miniato. "I do not know anything about the sea, but I dislike people who make difficulties and talk to me of bad weather when I mean to go anywhere. Do you understand?"

"We will try to content your excellency," answered Ruggiero quietly.

"Good. We shall see."

So Ruggiero went away to find the Son of the Fool, and the Cripple, and to engage them for the summer, and to deliver to his brother the message from the Marchesa di Mola. The reason why Ruggiero did not take Sebastiano as one of his own crew was a simple one. There lived and still lives at Sorrento, a certain old man known as the Greek. The Greek is old and infirm and has a vicious predilection for wine and cards, so that he is quite unfit for the sea. But he owns a couple of smart sailing boats and gets a living by letting them to strangers. It is necessary, however, to have at least one perfectly reliable man in charge of each, and so soon as the Children of the King had returned from their last long voyage the Greek had engaged them both for this purpose, as being in every way superior to the common run of boatmen who hung about the place waiting for jobs. It was consequently impossible that the two brothers could be in the same boat's crew during the summer.

Ruggiero found the Cripple asleep in the shade, having been out all night fishing, and the Son of the Fool was seated not far from him, plaiting sinnet for gaskets. The two were inseparable, so far as their varied life permitted them to be together, and were generally to be found in the same crew. Average able seamen both, much of the same height and build, broad, heavy fellows good at the oar, peaceable and uncomplaining.

While Ruggiero was talking with the one who was awake, his own brother appeared, and Ruggiero gave him the message, whereupon Sebastiano went off to array himself in his best before presenting himself to the Marchesa di Mola. The Son of the Fool gathered up his work.

"Mola?" he repeated in a tone of inquiry.

Ruggiero nodded carelessly.

"A Sicilian lady who has a cutter?"

"Yes."

"Her daughter is going to marry a certain Conte di San Miniato - a great signore - of those without soldi."

The sailor coiled the plaited sinnet neatly over his bare arm, but looked up as Ruggiero uttered an exclamation.

"What is the matter with you?" he asked.

Ruggiero's face was quite red and his broad chest heaved as he bit his lip and thrust his hands into his pockets. His companion repeated his question.

"Nothing is the matter," answered Ruggiero. "Wake up the Cripple and see if there is everything for rigging the boat. We must have her out this afternoon. The Conte di San Miniato of whom you speak is our signore."

"Oh! I understand!" exclaimed the Son of the Fool. "Well - you need not be so anxious. I daresay it is not true that he has no money, and at all events the Greek will pay us."

"Of course, the Greek will pay us," answered Ruggiero thoughtfully. "I will be back in half an hour," he added, turning away abruptly.

He walked rapidly up the steep paved ascent which leads through the narrow gorge from the small beach to the town above. A few minutes later he entered the chemist's shop for the first time in his life in search of medicine for himself. He took off his cap and looked about him with some curiosity, eying the long rows of old-fashioned majolica drug jars, and the stock of bottles of all colours and labels in the glass cases. The chemist was a worthy old creature with a white beard and solemn ways.

"What do you want?" he inquired.

"A little medicine, but good," answered Ruggiero, looking critically along the shelves, as though to select a remedy. "A little of the best," he added, jingling a few silver coins in his pockets and wondering how much the stuff would cost.

"But what kind of medicine?" asked the old man. "Do you feel ill? Where?"

"Here," answered Ruggiero bringing his heavy bony hand down upon his huge chest with a noise that made the chemist start, and then chuckle.

"Just there, eh?" said the latter ironically. "You have the health of a horse. Go to dinner."

"I tell you it is there," returned Ruggiero. "Sometimes it is quite quiet, as it is now, but sometimes it jumps and threshes like a dolphin at sea."

"H'm! The heart, eh?" The old man came round his counter and applied his ear to Ruggiero's breast. "Regular as a steam engine," he said. "When does it jump, as you call it? When you go up hill?"

Ruggiero laughed.

"Am I old or fat?" he inquired contemptuously. "It happened first this morning. I was waiting in the hotel and a lady came by and spoke to me - about a certain boat."

"A lady? H'm! Young perhaps, and pretty?"

"That is my business. Then half an hour later I was talking to the Son of the Fool. You know him I daresay. And it began to jump again, and I said to myself, '"Health is the first thing," as the old people say.' So I came for the medicine."

The chemist chuckled audibly.

"And what were you talking about?" he asked. "The lady?"

"It is true," answered Ruggiero in a tone of reflection. "The Son of the Fool was telling me that the lady is to marry my signore."

"And you want medicine!" cried the old man, laughing aloud. "Imbecile! Have you never been in love?"

Ruggiero stared at him.

"Eh! A girl here and there - in Buenos Ayres, in New Orleans - what has that to do with it? You - what the malora - the plague - are you talking about? Eh? Explain a little."

"You had better go back to Buenos Ayres, or to some other place where you will not see the lady any more," said the chemist. "You are in love with her. That is all the matter."

"I, with a gran' signora, a great lady! You are crazy, Don Ciccio!"

"Crazy or not - tell me to-morrow whether your heart does not beat every time she looks at you. As for her being a great lady - we are men, and they are women."

The chemist had socialistic ideas of his own.

"To please you," said Ruggiero, "I will go and see her now, and I will be back in an hour to tell you that you do not understand your business.

My brother is to go there at twelve and I will go with him. Of course I shall see her."

He turned to go, but stopped suddenly on the threshold and came back.

"There!" he cried triumphantly. "There it is again, but not so hard this time. Is the lady here, now?" He pushed his chest against the old man's ear.

"Madonna mia! What a machine!" exclaimed the latter, after listening a moment. "If I had a heart like that!"

"Now you see for yourself," said Ruggiero. "I want the best medicine."

But again the chemist broke into a laugh.

"Medicine! A medicine for love! Do you not see that it began to beat at the thought of seeing her? Go and try it, as you proposed. Then you will understand."

"I understand that you are crazy. But I will try it all the same."

Thereupon Ruggiero strode out of the shop without further words, considerably disappointed and displeased with the result of the interview. The chemist apparently took him for a fool. It was absurd to suppose that the sight of any woman, or the mention of any woman, could make a man's heart behave in such a way, and yet he was obliged to admit that the coincidence was undeniable.

He found his brother just coming out of the house in which they lodged, arrayed at all points exactly like himself. Sebastiano's young beard was not quite so thick, his eyes were a little softer, his movements a trifle less energetically direct than Ruggiero's, and he was, perhaps, an inch shorter; but the resemblance was extraordinary and would have struck any one.

They were admitted to the presence of the Marchesa di Mola in due time. She lay in a deep chair under the arches of her terrace, shaded by brown linen curtains, languid, idle, indifferent as ever.

"Beatrice!" she called in a lazy tone, as the two men stood still at a respectful distance, waiting to be addressed.

But instead of Beatrice, a maid appeared at a door at the other end of the terrace - a fresh young thing with rosy cheeks, brown hair, sparkling black eyes and a pretty figure.

"Call Donna Beatrice," said the Marchesa. Then, as though exhausted by the effort of speaking she closed her eyes and waited.

The maid cast a quick glance at the two handsome sailors and disappeared again. Ruggiero and Sebastiano stood motionless, only their eyes turning from side to side and examining everything with the curiosity habitual in seamen.

Presently Beatrice entered, looked at them both for a moment and then went up to her mother.

"It is for the boat, mamma," she said. "Do you wish me to arrange about it?"

"Of course," answered the Marchesa opening her eyes and immediately shutting them again.

Beatrice stepped aside and beckoned the two men to her. To Ruggiero's infinite surprise, he again felt the blood rushing to his face, and his heart began to pound his ribs like a fuller's hammer. He glanced at his brother and saw that he was perfectly self-possessed. Beatrice looked from one to the other in perplexity.

"You are so much alike!" she exclaimed. "With which of you did I speak this morning?"

"With me, Eccellenza," said Ruggiero, whose own voice sounded strangely in his ears. "And this is my brother," he added.

The arrangement was soon made, but during the short interchange of questions and answers Ruggiero could not take his eyes from Beatrice's face. Possibly he was not even aware that it was rude to stare at a lady, for his education had not been got in places where ladies are often seen, or manners frequently discussed. But Beatrice did not seem at all disturbed by the scrutiny, though she was quite aware of its pertinacity. A woman who has beauty in any degree rarely resents the genuine and unconcealed admiration of the vulgar. On the contrary, as the young girl dismissed the men, she smiled graciously upon them both, and perhaps a little the more upon Ruggiero, though there was not much to choose.

Neither of them spoke as they descended the stairs of the hotel, and went out through the garden to the gate. When they were in the square beyond Ruggiero stopped. Sebastiano stood still also and looked at him.

"Does your heart ever jump and turn somersaults and get into your mouth, when you look at a woman, Bastianello?" he asked.

"No. Does yours?"

"Yes. Just now."

"I saw her, too," answered Sebastiano. "It is true that she is very fresh and pretty, and uncommonly clean. Eh - the devil! If you like her, ask for her. The maid of a Marchesa is sure to have money and to be a respectable girl."

Ruggiero was silent for a moment and looked at his brother with an odd expression, as though he were going to say something. Unfortunately for him, for Sebastiano, for the maid, for Beatrice, and for the count of San Miniato, too, he said nothing. Instead, he produced half a cigar from his cap, and two sulphur matches, and incontinently began to smoke.

"It is lucky that both boats are engaged on the same day," observed Sebastiano. "The Greek will be pleased. He will play all the numbers at the lottery."

"And get very drunk to-night," added Ruggiero with contempt.

"Of course. But he is a good padrone, everybody says, and does not cheat his men."

"I hope not."

By and by the two went down to the beach again, and Sebastiano looked about him for a crew. The Marchesa wanted four men in her boat, or even five, and Sebastiano picked out at once the Gull, the Son of the American, Black Rag - otherwise known as Saint Peter from his resemblance to the pictures of the Apostle as a fisherman - and the Deaf Man. The latter is a fellow of strange ways, who lost his hearing from falling into the water in winter when overheated, and who has almost lost the power of speech in consequence, but a good sailor withal, tough, untiring, and patient.

They all set to work with a good will, and before four o'clock that day the two boats were launched, ballasted and rigged, the sails were bent to the yards and the brasses polished, so that Ruggiero and Sebastiano went up to their respective masters to ask if there were any orders for the afternoon.

F. Marion Crawford

CHAPTER IV

Ruggiero found out before long that his master for the summer was eccentric in his habits, judging from the Sorrentine point of view in regard to order and punctuality. Ruggiero's experience of fine gentlemen was limited indeed, but he could not believe that they all behaved like San Miniato, whose temper was apparently as changeable as his tastes. Sometimes he went to bed at nine o'clock and rose at dawn. Sometimes on the other hand he got up at seven in the evening and went to bed by daylight. Sometimes everything Ruggiero did was right, and sometimes everything was wrong. There were days when the Count could not be induced to move from the Marchesa di Mola's terrace between noon and midnight or later, and again there were days when he went off in his boat in the morning and did not return until the last stragglers on the terrace of the hotel were ready to go to bed. He was irregular even in playing, which was after all his chief pastime. Possibly he knew of reasons why it should be good to gamble on one day and not upon another. Then he had his fits of amateur seamanship, when he would insist upon taking the tiller from Ruggiero's hand. The latter, on such occasions, remained perched upon the stern in case of an emergency. San Miniato was a thorough landsman and never understood why the wind always seemed to change, or die away, or do something unexpected so soon as he began to steer the boat. From time to time Ruggiero, by way of a mild hint, held up his palm to the breeze, but San Miniato did not know what the action meant. Ruggiero trimmed the sails to suit the course chosen by his master as well as possible, but straightway the boat was up in the wind again if she had been going free, or was falling off if the tacks were down and the sheets well aft. San Miniato was one of those men who seem quite incapable of doing anything sensible from the moment they leave the land till they touch it again, when their normal common sense returns, and they once more become human beings.

On the other hand nothing frightened him, though he could not swim a stroke. More than once Ruggiero allowed him almost to upset the boat in a squall, and more than once, when, steering himself, and when there was a fresh breeze, drove her till the seas broke over the bows, and the green water came in over the lee gunwale - just to see whether the Count would change colour. In this, however, he was disappointed. San Miniato's temper might change and his tastes might be as variable as the moon, or the weather, but his face rarely expressed anything of what he felt, and if he felt anything at such times it was assuredly not fear. He had good qualities, and courage was one of them, if courage may be called a quality at all. Ruggiero was not at all sure that his new master liked the sea, and it is possible that the Count was not sure of the fact himself; but for the time, it suited him to sail as much as possible, because Beatrice Granmichele was fond of it, and would therefore amuse herself with excursions hither and thither during the summer. As her mother rarely accompanied her, San Miniato could not, according to the customs of the country, join her in her boat, and the next best thing was to keep one for himself and to be as often as possible alongside of her, and ready to go ashore with her if she took a fancy to land in some quiet spot.

The Marchesa di Mola, having quite made up her mind that her daughter should marry San Miniato, and being almost too indolent about minor matters to care for appearances, would have allowed the two to be together from morning till night under the very least shadow of a chaperon's supervision, if Beatrice herself had shown a greater inclination for San Miniato's society than she actually did. But Beatrice was the only one of the party who had arrived at no distinct determination in the matter. San Miniato attracted her, and was very well in his way, but that was all. Amidst the shoals of migratory Neapolitans with magnificent titles and slender purses, who appeared, disported themselves and disappeared again, at the summer resort, it was quite possible that one might be found with more to recommend him than San Miniato could boast. Most of them were livelier than he, and certainly all were noisier. Many of them had very bright black eyes, which Beatrice liked, and they were all dressed a little beyond the extreme of the fashion, a fact of which she was too young to understand the psychological value in judging of men. Some of them sang very prettily, and San Miniato did not possess any similar accomplishment. Indeed, in the young girl's opinion, he approached dangerously near to being a "serious" man, as the Italians express it, and but for his known love of gambling he might have seemed to her altogether too dull a personage to be thought of as a possible husband. It is not easy to define exactly what is meant in Italian by a "serious" man. The word does not exactly translate the French equivalent, still less the English one. It means something in the nature of a Philistine with a little admixture of Ciceronism - pass the word - and a dash of Cato Censor to sour the whole - a delight to school-masterly spirits, a terror to lively damsels, the laughing-stock of the worldly wise and only just too wise to find a congenial atmosphere in the every-day world. However, as San Miniato just escaped the application of the adjective I have been trying to translate, it is enough to say that he was not exactly a "serious man," being excluded from that variety of the species by his passion for play, which was dominant, and by the incidents of his past history, which had not been dull.

It is true that a liking for cards and a reputation for success gained in former love affairs are not in any sense a substitute for the outward and attractive expressions of a genuine and present passion, but they are better than nothing when they serve to combat such a formidable imputation as that of "seriousness." Anything is better than that, and as Beatrice Granmichele was inclined to like the man without knowing why, she made the most of the few stories about him which reached her maiden ears, and of his taste for gaming, in order to render him interesting in her own eyes. He did, indeed, make more or less pretty speeches to her from time to time, of a cheerfully complimentary character when he had won money, of a gracefully melancholy nature when he had lost, but she was far too womanly not to miss something very essential in what he said and in his way of saying it. A woman may love flattery ever so much and have ever so strong a moral absorbent system with which to digest it; she does not hate banality the less. There is no such word as banality in the English tongue, but there might be, and if there were, it would mean that peculiarly tasteless and saltless nature of actions and speeches done and delivered by persons who are born dull, or who are mentally exhausted, or are absent-minded, or very shy, but who, in spite of natural or accidental disadvantages are determined to make themselves agreeable. The standard of banality differs indeed for every woman, and with every woman for almost every hour of the day, and men of the world who husband their worldly resources are aware of the fact. Angelina at three in the afternoon, fresh from rest and luncheon - if both agree with her - is wreathed in smiles at a little speech of Edwin's which would taste like sweet camomile tea after dry champagne, at three in the morning, when the Hungarian music is ringing madly in her ears and there are only two more waltzes on the programme. Music, dancing, lights and heat are to a woman of the world what strong drinks are to a normal man; they may not intoxicate, but they change the humour. Fortunately for San Miniato the young lady whom he wished to marry was not just at present exposed to the action of those stimulants, and her moods were tolerably even. If he had been at all eloquent, the same style of eloquence would have done almost as well after dinner as after breakfast. But the secret springs of love speech were dried up in his brain by the haunting consciousness that much was expected of him. He had never before thought of marrying and had not yet in his life found himself for any length of time constantly face to face in conversation with a young girl, with limitations of propriety and the fear of failure before his eyes.

F. Marion Crawford

The situation was new and uncomfortable. He felt like a man who has got a hat which does not belong to him, which does not fit him and which will not stay on his head in a high wind. The consequence was that his talk lacked interest, and that he often did not talk at all. Nevertheless, he managed to show enough assiduity to keep himself continually in the foreground of Beatrice's thoughts. Being almost constantly present she could not easily forget him, and he held his ground with a determination which kept other men away. When a man can make a woman think of him half-a-dozen times a day and can prevent other men from taking his place when he is beside her, he is in a fair way to success.

On a certain evening San Miniato had a final interview with the Marchesa di Mola in which he expressed all that he felt for Beatrice, including a little more, and in which he described his not very prosperous financial condition with mitigated frankness. The Marchesa listened dreamily in the darkness on the terrace while her daughter played soft dance music in the dimly lighted room behind her. Beatrice probably had an idea of what was going on outside, upon the terrace, and was trying to make up her own mind. She played waltzes very prettily, as women who dance well generally do, if they play at all.

When San Miniato had finished, the Marchesa was silent for a few seconds. Then she tapped her companion twice upon the arm with her fan, in a way which would have seemed lazy in any one else, but which, for her, was unusually energetic.

"How well you say it all!" she exclaimed.

"And you consent, dear Marchesa?" asked the Count, with an eagerness not all feigned.

"You say it all so well! If I could say it half so well to Beatrice - there might be some possibility. But Beatrice is not like me - nor I like you - and so -"

She broke off in the middle of the sentence with an indolent little laugh.

"If she were like you," said San Miniato, "I would not hesitate long."

There was an intonation in his voice that pleased the middle-aged woman, as he had intended.

"What would you do?" she asked, fanning herself slowly in the dark.

"I would speak to her myself."

"Heavens!" Again the Marchesa laughed. The idea seemed eccentric enough in her eyes.

"Why not?"

"Why not? Dearest San Miniato, do not try to make me argue such insane questions with you. You know how lazy I am. I can never talk."

"A woman need not talk in order to be persuaded. It is enough that the man should. Let me try."

"I will shut my ears."

"I will kneel at your feet."

"I shall go to sleep."

"I could wake you."

"How?"

"By telling you that I mean to speak to Donna Beatrice myself."

"Such an idea would wake the dead!"

"So much the better. They would hear me."

"They would not help you, if they heard you," observed the Marchesa.

"They could at least bear witness to the answer I should receive."

"And suppose, dear friend, that the answer should not be what you wish, or expect - would you care to have witnesses, alive or dead?"

"Why should the answer be a negative?"

"Because," replied the Marchesa, turning her face directly to his, "because Beatrice is herself uncertain. You know well enough that no man should ever tell a woman he loves her until he is sure that she loves him. And that is not the only reason."

"Have you a better one?" asked San Miniato with a laugh.

"The impossibility of it all! Imagine, in our world, a man deliberately asking a young girl to marry him!"

San Miniato smiled, but the Marchesa could not see the expression of his face.

"We do not think it so impossible in Piedmont," he answered quietly.

"I am surprised at that." The lady's tone was rather cold.

"Are you? Why? We are less old-fashioned, that is all."

"And is it really done in - in good families?"

"Often," answered San Miniato, seeing his advantage and pressing it. "I could give you many instances without difficulty, within the last few years."

"The plan certainly saves the parents a great deal of trouble," observed the Marchesa, lazily shutting her eyes and fanning herself again.

"And it places the decision of the most vital question in life in the hands of the two beings most concerned."

San Miniato spoke rather sententiously, for he knew how to impress his companion and he meant to be impressive.

"No doubt," answered the Marchesa. "No doubt. But," she continued, bringing up the time-honoured argument, "the two young people most concerned are not always the people best able to judge of their own welfare."

"Of course they are not," assented San Miniato, readily enough, and abandoning the point which could be of no use to him. "Of course not. But, dearest Marchesa, since you have judged for us - and there is no one else to judge - do you not think that you might leave the rest in my hands? The mere question to be asked, you know, in the hope of a final answer - the mere technicality of love-making, with which you can only be familiar from the woman's point of view, and not from the man's, as I am. Not that I have had much experience -"

"You?" laughed the Marchesa, touching his hand with her fan. "You without much experience! But you are historical, dearest friend! Who does not know of your conquests?"

"I, at least, do not," answered San Miniato with well-affected modesty. "But that is not the question. Let us get back to it. This is my plan. The moon is full to-morrow and the weather is hot. We will all go in my boat to Tragara and dine on the rocks. It will be beautiful. Then after dinner we can walk about in the moonlight - slowly, not far from you, as at the end of this terrace. And while you are looking on I, in a low voice, will express my sincere feelings to Donna Beatrice, and ask the most important of all questions. Does not that please you? Is it not well combined?"

"But why must we take the trouble to go all the way to Capri? What sense is there in that?"

"Dearest Marchesa, you do not understand! Consider the surroundings, the moonlight, the water rippling against the rocks, the soft breeze - a little music, too, such as a pair of mandolins and a guitar, which we could send over - all these things are in my favour."

"Why?" asked the Marchesa, not understanding in the least how he could attach so much value to things which seemed to her unappreciative mind to be perfectly indifferent.

"Besides," she added, "if you want to give a party, you can illuminate the garden of the hotel with Chinese lanterns. That would be much prettier than to picnic on uncomfortable rocks out in the sea with nothing but cold things to eat and only the moon for an illumination. I am sure Beatrice would like it much better."

San Miniato laughed.

"What a prosaic person you are!" he exclaimed. "Can you not imagine that a young girl's disposition may be softened by moonlight, mandolins and night breezes?"

"No. I never understood that. And after all if you want moonlight you can have it here. If it shines at Capri it will shine at Sorrento. At least it seems to me so."

"No, dearest Marchesa," answered San Miniato triumphantly. "There you are mistaken."

"About the moon?"

"Yes, about the moon. When it rises we do not see it here, on account of the mountains behind us."

"But I have often seen the moon here, from this very place," objected the Marchesa. "I am sure it is not a week ago that I saw it. You do not mean to tell me that there are two moons, and that yours is different from mine!"

"Very nearly. This at least I say. When the moon is full we can see it rise from Tragara, and we can not see it from this place."

"How inexplicable nature is!" exclaimed the Marchesa fanning herself lazily. "I will not try to understand the moon any more. It tires me. A lemonade, San Miniato - ring for a lemonade. I am utterly exhausted."

"Shall I ask Donna Beatrice's opinion about Tragara?" inquired San Miniato rising.

"Oh yes! Anything - only do not argue with me. I cannot bear it. I suppose you will put me into that terrible boat and make me sit in it for hours and hours, until all my bones are broken, and then you will give me cold macaroni and dry bread and warm wine and water, and the sailors will eat garlic, and it will be insufferable and you will call it divine. And of course Beatrice will be so wretched that she will not listen to a word you say, and will certainly refuse you without hesitation. A lemonade, San Miniato, for the love of heaven! My throat is parched with this talking."

When the Marchesa had got what she wanted, San Miniato sat down beside Beatrice at the piano, in the sitting room.

"Donna Beatrice gentilissima," he began, "will you deign to tell me whether you prefer the moon to Chinese lanterns, or Chinese lanterns to the moon?"

"To wear?" asked the young girl with a laugh.

"If you please, of course. Anything would be becoming to you

- but I mean as a question of light. Would you prefer a dinner by moonlight on the rocks of Tragara with a couple of mandolins in the distance, or would you like better a party in the hotel gardens with an illumination of paper lanterns? It is a most important question, I assure you, and must be decided very quickly, because the moon is full to-morrow."

"What a ridiculous question!" exclaimed Beatrice, laughing again.

"Why ridiculous?"

"Because you ought to know the answer well enough. Imagine comparing the moon with Chinese lanterns!"

"Your mother prefers the latter."

"Oh, mamma - of course! She is so practical. She would prefer carriage lamps on the trees - gas if possible! When are we going to Tragara? Where is it? Which boat shall we take? Oh, it is too delightful! Can we not go to-night?"

"We can do anything which Donna Beatrice likes," answered San Miniato. "But if you will listen to me, I will explain why to-morrow would be better. In the first place, we have dined once this evening, so that we could not dine again."

"We could call it supper," suggested Beatrice.

"Of course we could, if we could eat it at all. But it is also ten o'clock, and we could not get to Tragara before one or two in the morning. Lastly, your mother would not go."

"Will she go to-morrow?" asked Beatrice with sudden anxiety. "Have you asked her?"

"She will go," answered San Miniato confidently. "We must make her comfortable. That is the principal thing."

"Yes. She shall have her maid and we must take a chair for her to sit in, and another to carry her, and two porters, and a lamp, and a table, and a servant to wait on her. And she will want champagne, well iced, and a carpet for her feet, and a screen to keep the wind from her, if there is any, and several more things which I shall remember. But I know all about it, for we once made a little excursion from Taormina and dined out of doors, and I know exactly what she wants."

"Very well, she shall have everything," said San Miniato smiling at the catalogue of the Marchesa's wants. "If she will only go, we will do all we can."

"When it is time, let the two porters come in here with the chair and take her away," answered Beatrice. "Dear mamma! She will be much too lazy to resist. What fun it will be!"

And everything was done as Beatrice had wished. San Miniato made a list of things absolutely indispensable to the Marchesa. The number of articles was about two hundred and their bulk filled a boat which was despatched early in the following afternoon to be rowed over to Tragara and unloaded before the party arrived.

Ruggiero and his brother worked hard at the preparations, silent, untiring and efficient as usual, but delighted in their hearts at the prospect of something less monotonous than the daily sail or the daily row within sight of Sorrento. To men who have knocked about the sea for years, from Santa Cruz to Sebastopol, the daily life of a sailor on a little pleasure boat lacks interest, and if circumstances had been, different Ruggiero would probably have shipped before now as boatswain on board one of the neat schooners which are yearly built at the Piano di Sorrento, to be sold with their cargoes of salt as soon as they reach Buenos Ayres. But Ruggiero had contracted that malady of the heart which had taken him to the chemist's for the first time in his life, and which materially hindered the formation of any plan by which he might be obliged to leave his present situation. Moreover the disease showed no signs of yielding; on the contrary, the action of the vital organ concerned became more and more spasmodic and alarming, while its possessor grew daily leaner and more silent.

The last package had been taken down, the last of the score of articles which the Marchesa was sure to want with her in the sail boat before she reached the spot where the main cargo of comforts would be waiting; the last sandwich, the last box of sweetmeats, the iced lemonade, the wraps and the parasols were all stowed away in their places. Then San Miniato went to fetch the Marchesa, marshalling in his two porters with their chair between them.

"Dearest Marchesa," said the Count, "if you will give yourself the trouble to sit in this chair, I will promise that no further exertion shall be required of you."

The Marchesa di Mola looked up with a glance of sleepy astonishment.

"And why in that chair, dearest friend? I am so comfortable here. And why have you brought those two men with you?"

"Have you forgotten our dinner at Tragara?" asked San Miniato.

"Tragara!" gasped the Marchesa. "You are not going to take me to Tragara! Good heavens! I am utterly exhausted! I shall die before we get to the boat."

"Altro e parlar di morte - altro e morire," laughed San Miniato, quoting the famous song. "It is one thing to talk of death, it is quite another to die. Only this little favour Marchesa gentilissima - to seat yourself in this chair. We will do the rest."

"Without a hat? Just as I am? Impossible! Come in an hour - then I shall be ready. My maid, San Miniato - send for Teresina. Dio mio! I can never go! Go without us, dearest friend - go and dine on your hideous rocks and leave us the little comfort we need so much!"

But protestations were vain. Teresina appeared and fastened the hat of the period upon her mistress's head. The hat of the period chanced to be a one-sided monstrosity at that time, something between a cart wheel, an umbrella and a flower garden, depending for its stability upon the proper position of several solid skewers, apparently stuck through the head of the wearer. This headpiece having been adjusted the Marchesa asked for a cigarette, lighted it and looked about her.

"It is really too much!" she exclaimed. "Button my gloves, Teresina. I shall not go after all, not even to please you, dearest friend. What a place of torture this world is! How right we are to try and get a comfortable stall in the next! Go away, San Miniato. It is quite useless."

But San Miniato knew what he was doing. With gentle strength he made her rise from her seat and placed her in the chair. The porters lifted their burden, settled the straps upon their shoulders, the man in front glanced back at the man behind, both nodded and marched away.

"This is too awful!" sighed the Marchesa, as she was carried out of thedoor of the sitting room. "How can you have the heart, dearest friend! An invalid like me! And I was supremely comfortable where I was."

But at this point Beatrice appeared and joined the procession, radiant, fresh as a fragrant wood-flower, full of life as a young bird. Behind her came Teresina, the maid, necessary at every minute for the Marchesa's comfort, her pink young cheeks flushed with pleasure and her eyes sparkling with anticipation, fastening on her hat as she walked.

"I was never so happy in my life," laughed Beatrice. "And to think that you have really captured mamma in spite of herself! Oh, mamma, you will enjoy it so much! I promise you shall.

There is iced champagne, and the foot warmer and the marrons glaces and the lamp and everything you like - and quails stuffed with truffles, besides. Now do be happy and let us enjoy ourselves!"

"But where are all these things?" asked the Marchesa. "I shall believe when I see."

"Everything is at Tragara already," answered Beatrice tripping down the stairs beside her mother's chair. "And we really will enjoy ourselves," she added, turning her head with a bewitching smile, and looking back at San Miniato. "What a general you are!"

"If you could convince the Minister of War of that undoubted fact, you would be conferring the greatest possible favour upon me," said the Count. "He would have no trouble in persuading me to return to the army as commander-in-chief, though I left the service as a captain."

So they went down the long winding way cut through the soft tufo rock and found the boat waiting for them by the little landing. The Marchesa actually took the trouble to step on board instead of trusting herself to the strong arms of Ruggiero. Beatrice followed her. As she set her foot on the gunwale Ruggiero held up his hand towards her to help her. It was not the first time this duty had fallen to him, but she was more radiantly fresh to-day than he had ever seen her before, and the spasm that seemed to crush his heart for a moment was more violent than usual. His strong joints trembled at her light touch and his face turned white. She felt that his hand shook and she glanced at him when she stood in the boat.

"Are you ill, Ruggiero?" she asked, in a kindly tone.

"No, Excellency," he answered in a low voice that was far from steady, while the shadow of a despairing smile flickered over his features.

He put up his hand to help Teresina, the maid. She pressed it hard as she jumped down, and smiled with much intention at the handsome sailor. But she got no answer for her look, and he turned away and shoved the boat off the little stone pier. Bastianello was watching them both, and wishing himself in Ruggiero's place. But Ruggiero, as he believed, had loved the pretty Teresina first, and Ruggiero had the first right to win her if he could.

So the boat shot out upon the crisping water into the light afternoon breeze, and up went foresail and mainsail and jib, and away she went on the port tack, San Miniato steering and talking to Beatrice - which things are not to be done together with advantage - the Marchesa lying back in a cane rocking-chair and thinking of nothing, while Teresina held the parasol over her mistress's head and shot bright glances at the sailors forward. And Ruggiero and Bastianello sat side by side amidships looking out at the gleaming sea to windward.

"What hast thou?" asked Bastianello in a low voice.

"The pain," answered his brother.

"Why let thyself be consumed by it? Ask her in marriage. The Marchesa will give her to thee."

"Better to die! Thou dost not know all."

"That may be," said Bastianello with a sigh.

And he slowly began to fake down the slack of the main halyard on the thwart, twisting the coil slowly and thoughtfully as it grew under his broad hands, till the rope lay in a perfectly smooth disk beside him. But Ruggiero changed his position and gazed steadily at Beatrice's changing face while San Miniato talked to her.

So the boat sped on and many of those on board misunderstood each other, and some did not understand themselves. But what was most clear to all before long was that San Miniato could not make love and steer his trick at the same time.

"Are we going to Castellamare?" asked Bastianello in a low voice as the boat fell off more and more under the Count's careless steering.

Ruggiero started. For the first time in his life he had forgotten that he was at sea.

CHAPTER V

San Miniato did not possess that peculiar and common form of vanity which makes a man sensitive about doing badly what he has never learned to do at all. He laughed when Ruggiero advised him to luff a little, and he did as he was told. But Ruggiero came aft and perched himself on the stern in order to be at hand in case his master committed another flagrant breach of seamanship.

"You will certainly take us to the bottom of the bay instead of to Tragara," observed the Marchesa languidly. "But then at least my discomforts will be over for ever. Of course there is no lemonade on board. Teresina, I want lemonade."

In an instant Bastianello produced a decanter out of a bucket of snow and brought it aft with a glass. The Marchesa smiled.

"You do things very well, dearest friend," she said, and moistened her lips in the cold liquid.

"Donna Beatrice has had more to do with providing for your comfort than I," answered the Count.

The Marchesa smiled lazily, sipped about a teaspoonful from the glass and handed it to her maid.

"Drink, Teresina," she said. "It will refresh you."

The girl drank eagerly.

F. Marion Crawford

"You see," said the Marchesa, "I can think of the comfort of others as well as of my own."

San Miniato smiled politely and Beatrice laughed. Her laughter hurt the silent sailor perched behind her, as though a glass had been broken in his face. How could she be so gay when his heart was beating so hard for her? He drew his breath sharply and looked out to sea, as many a heart-broken man has looked across that fair water since woman first learned that men's hearts could break.

It was a wonderful afternoon. The sun was already low, rolling down to his western bath behind Capo Miseno, northernmost of all his daily plunges in the year; and as he sank, the colours he had painted on the hills at dawn returned behind him, richer and deeper and rarer for the heat he had given them all day. There, like a mass of fruit and flowers in a red gold bowl, Sorrento lay in the basin of the surrounding mountains, all gilded above and full of rich shadows below. Over all, the great Santangelo raised his misty head against the pale green eastern sky, gazing down at the life below, at the living land and the living sea, and remembering, perhaps, the silent days before life was, or looking forward to the night to come in which there will be no life left any more. For who shall tell me that the earth herself may not be a living, thinking, feeling being, on whose not unkindly bosom we wear out our little lives, but whose high loves are with the stars, beyond our sight, and her voice too deep and musical for ears used to our shrill human speech? Who shall say surely that she is not conscious of our presence, of some of our doings when we tear her breast and lay burdens upon her neck and plough up her fair skin with our hideous works, or when we touch her kindly and love her, and plant sweet flowers in soft places? Who shall know and teach us that the summer breeze is not her breath, the storm the sobbing of her passion, the rain her woman's tears - that she is not alive, loving and suffering, as we all have been, are, or would be, but greater than we as the star she loves somewhere is greater and stronger than herself? And we live upon her, and feed on her and all die and are taken back into her whence we came, wondering much of the truth that is hidden, learning perhaps at last the great secret she keeps so well. Her life, too, will end some day, her last blossom will have bloomed alone, her last tears will have fallen upon her own bosom, her last sob will have rent the air, and the beautiful earth will be dead for ever, borne on in the sweep of the race that will never end, borne along yet a few ages, till her sweet body turns to star-dust in the great emptiness of a night without morning.

But Ruggiero, plain strong man of the people, hard-handed sailor, was not thinking of any of these things as he sat in his narrow place on the stern behind his master, mechanically guiding the tiller in the latter's unconscious hand, while he gazed silently at Beatrice's face, now turned towards him in conversation, now half averted as she looked down or out to sea. Ruggiero listened, too, to the talk, though he did not understand all the fine words Beatrice and San Miniato used. If he had never been away from the coast, the probability is that he would have understood nothing at all; but in his long voyages he had been thrown with men of other parts of Italy and had picked up a smattering of what Neapolitans call Italian, to distinguish it from their own speech. Even as it was, the most part of what they said escaped him, because they seemed to think so very differently from him about simple matters, and to be so heartily amused at what seemed so dull to him. And he began to feel that the hurt he had was deep and not to be healed, while he reflected that he was undoubtedly mad, since he loved this lady so much while understanding her so little. The mere feeling that she could talk and take pleasure in talking beyond his comprehension wounded him, as a sensitive half-grown boy sometimes suffers real pain when his boyishness shows itself among men.

Why, for instance, did the young girl's cheek flush and her eyes sparkle, when San Miniato talked of Paris? Paris was in France. Ruggiero knew that. But he had often heard that it was not so big a place as London, where he had been. Therefore Beatrice must have some other reason for liking it. Most probably she loved a Frenchman, and Ruggiero hated Frenchmen with all his heart. Then they talked about the theatre and Beatrice was evidently interested. Ruggiero had once seen a puppet show and had not found it at all funny. The theatre was only a big puppet show, and he could pay for a seat there if he pleased; but he did not please, because he was sure that it would not amuse him to go. Why should Beatrice like the theatre? And she liked the races at Naples, too, and those at Paris much better. Why? Everybody knew that one horse could run faster than another, without trying it, but it could not matter a straw which of two, or twenty, got to the goal first. Horses were not boats. Now there was sense in a boat race, or a yacht race, or a steamer race. But a horse! He might be first to-day, and to-morrow if he had not enough to eat he might be last. Was a horse a Christian? You could not count upon him. And then they began to talk of love and Ruggiero's heart stood still, for that, at least, he could understand.

"Love!" laughed Beatrice, repeating the word. "It always makes one laugh. Were you ever in love, mamma?"

The Marchesa turned her head slowly, and lifted her sleepy eyes to look at her daughter, before she answered.

"No," she said lazily. "I was never in love. But you are far too young to talk of such things."

"San Miniato says that love is for the young and friendship for the old."

"Love," said San Miniato, "is a necessary evil, but it is also the greatest source of happiness."

"What a fine phrase!" exclaimed Beatrice. "You must be a professor in disguise."

"A professor of love?" asked the Count with a very well executed look of tenderness which did not escape Ruggiero.

"Hush, for the love of heaven!" interposed the Marchesa. "This is too dreadful!"

"We were not talking of the love of heaven," answered Beatrice mischievously.

"I was thinking at least of a love that could make any place a heaven," said San Miniato, again helping his lack of originality with his eyes.

Ruggiero reflected that it would be but the affair of a second to unship the heavy brass tiller and bring it down once on the top of his master's skull. Once would be enough.

"Whose love?" asked Beatrice innocently.

San Miniato looked at her again, then turned away his eyes and sighed audibly.

"Well?" asked Beatrice. "Will you answer. I do not understand that language. Whose love would make any place - Timbuctoo, for instance - a heaven for you?"

"Discretion is the only virtue a man ought to exhibit whenever he has a chance," said San Miniato.

"Perhaps. But even that should be shown without ostentation." Beatrice laughed. "And you are decidedly ostentatious at the present moment. It would interest mamma and me very much to know the object of your affections."

"Beatrice!" exclaimed the Marchesa with affected horror.

"Yes, mamma," answered the young girl. "Here I am. Do you want some more lemonade?"

"She is quite insufferable," said the Marchesa to San Miniato, with a languid smile. "But really, San Miniato carissimo, this conversation - a young girl -"

Ruggiero wondered what she found so obnoxious in the words that had been spoken. He also wondered how long it would take San Miniato to drown if he were dropped overboard in the wake of the boat.

"If that is your opinion of your daughter," said the latter, "we shall hardly agree. Now I maintain that Donna Beatrice is the contrary of insufferable - the most extreme of contraries. In the first place -"

"She is very pretty," said Beatrice demurely.

"I was not going to say that," laughed San Miniato.

"Ah? Then say something else."

"I will. Donna Beatrice has two gifts, at least, which make it impossible that she should ever be insufferable, even when her beauty is gone."

"Dio mio!" ejaculated the young girl. "The compliments are beginning in good earnest!"

"It was time," said San Miniato, "since your mother -"

"Dear Count," interrupted Beatrice, "do not talk any more about mamma. I am anxious to get at the compliments. Do pray let your indiscretion be as ostentatious as possible. I cannot wait another second."

"No need of waiting," answered San Miniato, again addressing himself to the Marchesa. "Donna Beatrice has two great gifts. She is kind, and she has charm."

There being no exact equivalent for the word "charm" in the Italian language, San Miniato used the French. Ruggiero began to puzzle his brains, asking himself what this foreign virtue could be which his master estimated so highly. He also thought it very strange that Beatrice should have said of herself that she was pretty, and still stranger that San Miniato should not have said it.

"Is that all?" asked Beatrice. "I need not have been in such a hurry to extract your compliments from you."

"If you had understood what I said," answered San Miniato unmoved, "you would see that no man could say more of a woman."

"Kind and charming! It is not much," laughed the young girl. "Unless you mean much more than you say - and I asked you to be indiscreet!"

"Kind hearts are rare enough in this world, Donna Beatrice, and as for charm -"

"What is charm?"

"It is what the violet has, and the camelia has not -"

"Heavens! Are you going to sigh to me in the language of flowers?"

"Beatrice! Beatrice!" cried the Marchesa, with the same affectation of horror as before.

"Dear mamma, are you uncomfortable? Oh no! I see now. You are horrified. Have I said anything dreadful?" she asked, turning to San Miniato.

"Anything dreadful? What an idea! Really, Marchesa carissima, I was just beginning to explain to Donna Beatrice what charm is, when you cut me short. I implore you to let me go on with my explanation."

"On condition that Beatrice makes no comments. Give me a cigarette, Teresina."

"The congregation will not interrupt the preacher before the benediction," said Beatrice folding her small hands on her knee, and looking down with a devout expression.

"Charm," began San Miniato, "is the something which some women possess, and which holds the men who love them -"

"Only those who love them?" interrupted Beatrice, looking up quickly.

"I thought," said the Marchesa, "that you were not to give us any comments." She dropped the words one or two at a time between the puffs of her cigarette.

"A question is not a comment, mamma. I ask for instruction."

"Go on, dearest friend," said her mother to the Count. "She is incorrigible."

"On the contrary, Donna Beatrice fills my empty head with ideas. The question was to the point. All men feel the charm of such women as all men smell the orange blossoms here in May -"

"The language of flowers again!" laughed Beatrice.

"You are so like a flower," answered San Miniato softly.

"Am I?" She laughed again, then grew grave and looked away.

Ruggiero's hand shook on the heavy tiller, and San Miniato, who supposed he was steering all the time, turned suddenly.

"What is the matter?" he asked.

"The rudder is draking, Excellency," answered Ruggiero.

"And what does that mean?" asked Beatrice.

"It means that the rudder trembles as the boat rises and falls with each sea, when there is a good breeze," answered Ruggiero.

"Is there any danger?" asked Beatrice indifferently.

"What danger could there be, Excellency?" asked the sailor.

"Because you are so pale, Ruggiero. What is the matter with you, to-day?"

"Nothing, Excellency."

"Ruggiero is in love," laughed San Miniato. "Is it not true, Ruggiero?"

But the sailor did not answer, though the hot blood came quickly to his face and stayed there a moment and then sank away again. He looked steadily at the dancing waves to windward, and set his lips tightly together.

"I would like to ask that sailor what he thinks of love and charm, and all the rest of it," said Beatrice. "His ideas would be interesting."

Ruggiero's blue eyes turned slowly upon her, with an odd expression. Then he looked away again.

"I will ask him," said San Miniato in a low voice. "Ruggiero!"

"Excellency!"

"We want to know what you think about love. What is the best quality a woman can have?"

"To be honest," answered Ruggiero promptly.

"And after that, what next?"

"To be beautiful."

"And then rich, I suppose?"

"It would be enough if she did not waste money."

"Honest, beautiful, and economical!" exclaimed Beatrice. "He does not say anything about charm, you see. I think his description is extremely good and to the point. Bravo, Ruggiero!"

His eyes met hers and gleamed rather fiercely for an instant.

"And how about charm, Ruggiero?" asked Beatrice mischievously.

"I do not speak French, Excellency," he answered.

"You should learn, because charm is a word one cannot say in Italian. I do not know how to say it in our language."

"Let me talk about flowers to him," said San Miniato. "I will make him understand. Which do you like better, Ruggiero, camelias or violets?"

"The camelia is a more lordly flower, Excellency, but for me I like the violets."

"Why?"

"Who knows? They make one think of so many things, Excellency. One would tire of camelias, but one would never be tired of violets. They have something - who knows?"

"That is it, Ruggiero," said San Miniato, delighted with the result of his experiment. "And charm is the same thing in a woman. One is never tired of it, and yet it is not honesty, nor beauty, nor economy."

"I understand, Excellency - e la femmina - it is the womanly."

"Bravo, Ruggiero!" exclaimed Beatrice again. "You are a man of heart. And if you found a woman who was honest and beautiful and economical and 'femmina,' as you say, would you love her?"

"Yes, Excellency, very much," answered Ruggiero. But his voice almost failed him.

"How much? Tell us."

Ruggiero was silent a moment. Then his eyes flashed suddenly as he looked down at her and his voice came ringing and strong.

"So much that I would pray that Christ and the sea would take her, rather than that another man should get her! Per Dio!"

There was such a vibration of strong passion in the words that Beatrice started a little and San Miniato looked up in surprise. Even the Marchesa vouchsafed the sailor a glance of indolent curiosity. Beatrice bent over to the Count and spoke in a low tone and in French.

"We must not tease him any more. He is in love and very much in earnest."

"So am I," answered San Miniato with a half successful attempt to seem emotional, which might have done well enough if it had no t come afterRuggiero's heartfelt speech.

"You!" laughed Beatrice. "You are never really in earnest. You only think you are, and that pleases you as well."

San Miniato bit his lip, for he was not pleased. Her answer augured ill for the success of the plan he meant to put into execution that very evening. He felt strongly incensed against Ruggiero, too, without in the least understanding the reason.

"You will find out some day, Donna Beatrice, that those who are most in earnest are not those who make the most passionate speeches."

"Ah! Is that true? How strange! I should have supposed that if a man said nothing it was because he had nothing to say. But you have such novel theories!"

"Is this discussion never to end?" asked the Marchesa, wearily lifting her hand as though in protest, and letting it fall again beside the other.

"It has only just begun, mamma," answered Beatrice cheerfully. "When San Miniato jumps into the sea and drowns himself in despair, you will know that the discussion is over."

"Beatrice! My child! What language!"

"Italian, mamma carissima. Italian with a little Sicilian, such as we speak."

"I am at your service, Donna Beatrice," said the Count. "Would you like me to drown myself immediately, or are you inclined for a little more conversation?"

Ruggiero had now taken the helm altogether. As San Miniato spoke he nodded to his brother who was forward, intimating that he meant to go about. He was certainly not in his normal frame of mind, for he had an evil thought at that moment. Fortunately for every one concerned the breeze was very light and was indeed dying away as the sun sank lower. They were already nearing the southernmost point of Capri, commonly called by sailors the Monaco, for what reason no one knows. To reach Tragara where the Faraglioni, or needles, rise out of the deep sea close to the rocky shore under the cliffs, it is necessary to go round the point. There was soon hardly any breeze at all, so that Bastianello and the other men shipped half-a-dozen oars and began to row. The operation of going about involved a change of places in so small a boat and the slight confusion had interrupted the conversation. A long silence followed, broken at last by the Marchesa's voice.

"A cigarette, Teresina, and some more lemonade. Are you still there, San Miniato carissimo? As I heard no more conversation I supposed you had drowned yourself as you proposed to do."

"Donna Beatrice is so kind as to put off the execution until after dinner."

"And shall we ever reach this dreadful place, and ever really dine?" asked the Marchesa.

"Before sunset," answered San Miniato. "And we shall dine at our usual hour."

"At least it will not be so hot as in the hotel, and after all it has not been very fatiguing."

"No," said the Count, "I fail to see how your exertions can have tired you much."

Ruggiero looked down at his master and at the fine lady as she lay listlessly extended in her cane chair, and he felt that in his heart he hated them both as much as he loved Beatrice, which was saying much. But he wondered how it was that less than half an hour earlier he had been ready to upset the boat and drown every one in it indiscriminately. Nevertheless he believed that if there had been a stiff breeze just then, enough for his purpose, he would have stopped the boat's way, and then put the helm hard up again, without slacking out a single sheet, and he knew the little craft well enough to be sure of what would have happened. Murderous intentions enough, as he thought of it all now, in the calm water under the great cliff from which tradition says that Tiberius shot delinquents into space from a catapult.

The men pulled hard by the lonely rocks, for the sun had almost set and they knew how sharp the stones are at Tragara, when one must tread them barefoot and burdened with hampers and kettles and all the paraphernalia of a picnic.

Then the light grew rich and deep, and the sea swallows shot from the misty heights, like arrows, into the calm purple air below, and skimmed and wheeled, and rose again, startled by the splash of the oars and the dull knock of them as they swung in the tholes. And the water was like a mirror in which all manner of rare and lovely things are reflected, with blots of liquid gold and sheen of soft-hued damask, and great handfuls of pearls and opals strewn between, and roses and petals of many kinds of flowers without names. And the air was full of the faint, salt odours that haunt the lonely places of the sea, sweet and bitter at once as the last days of a young life fading fast. Then the great needles rose gigantic from the depths to heaven, and beyond, through the mysterious, shadowy arch that pierces one of them, was opened the glorious vision of a distant cloud-lit water, and a single dark sail far away stood still, as it were, on the very edge of the world.

Beatrice leaned back and gazed at the scene, and her delicate nostrils expanded as she breathed. There was less colour in her face than there had been, and the long lashes half veiled her eyes. San Miniato watched her narrowly.

"How beautiful! How beautiful!" she exclaimed twice, after a long silence.

"It will be more beautiful still when the moon rises," said San Miniato. "I am glad you are pleased."

She liked the simple words better, perhaps, than some of his rather artificial speeches.

"Thank you," she said. "Thank you for bringing us here."

He had certainly taken a great deal of trouble, she thought, and it was the least she could do, to thank him as she did. But she was really grateful and for a moment she felt a sort of sympathy for him which she had not felt before. He, at least, understood that one could like something better in the world than the eternal terrace of a hotel with its stiff orange trees, its ugly lanterns and its everlasting gossip and chatter. He, at least, was a little unlike all those other people, beginning with her own mother, who think of self first, comfort second, and of others once a month or so, in the most favourable cases. Yet she wondered a little about his past life, and whether he had ever spoken to any woman with that ringing passion she had heard in Ruggiero's voice, with that flashing look she had seen in the sailor's bright blue eyes. It would be good to be spoken to like that. It would be good to see the colour in a man's face change, and come and go, red and white like life and death. It would be supremely good to be loved once, madly, passionately, with body, heart and soul, to the very breaking of all three - to be held in strong arms, to be kissed half to death.

She stopped, conscious that her mother would certainly not approve such thoughts, and well aware in her girlish heart that she did not approve them in herself. And then she smiled faintly. The man of her waking vision was not like San Miniato. He was more like Ruggiero, the poor sailor, who sat perched on the stern close behind her. She smiled uneasily at the idea, and then she thought seriously of it for a moment. If such a man as Ruggiero appeared, not as a sailor, but as a man of her own world, would he not be a very lovable person, would he not turn the heads of the languid ladies on the terrace of the hotel at Sorrento? The thought annoyed her. Ruggiero, poor fellow, would have given his good right arm to know that such a possibility had even crossed her reflections. But it was not probable that he ever would know it, and he sat in his place, silent and unmoved, steering the boat to her destination, and thinking of her.

It was not dusk when the boat was alongside of the low jagged rocks which lie between the landward needle and the cliffs, making a sort of rough platform in which there are here and there smooth flat places worn by the waves and often full of dry salt for a day or two after a storm. There, to the Marchesa's inexpressible relief, the numberless objects inscribed in the catalogue of her comforts were already arranged, and she suffered herself to be lifted from the boat and carried ashore by Ruggiero and his brother, without once murmuring or complaining of fatigue - a truly wonderful triumph for San Miniato's generalship.

There was the table, the screen, and the lamp, the chairs and the carpet - all the necessary furniture for the Marchesa's dining-room. And there at her place stood an immaculate individual in an evening coat and a white tie, ready and anxious to do her bidding. She surveyed the preparations with more satisfaction than she generally showed at anything. Then all at once her face fell.

"Good heavens, San Miniato carissimo," she cried, "you have forgotten the red pepper! It is all over! I shall eat nothing! I shall die in this place!"

"Pardon me, dearest Marchesa, I know your tastes. There is red pepper and also Tabasco on the table. Observe - here and here."

The Marchesa's brow cleared.

"Forgive me, dear friend," she said. "I am so dependent on these little things! You are an angel, a general and a man of heart."

"The man of your heart, I hope you mean to say," answered San Miniato, looking at Beatrice.

"Of course - anything you like - you are delightful. But I am dropping with fatigue. Let me sit down."

"You have forgotten nothing - not even the moon you promised me," said Beatrice, gazing with clasped hands at the great yellow shield as it slowly rose above the far south-eastern hills.

"I will never forget anything you ask me, Donna Beatrice," replied San Miniato in a low voice. Something told him that in the face of all nature's beauty, he must speak very simply, and he was right.

There is but one moment in the revolution of day and night which is more beautiful than the rising of the full moon at sunset, and that is the dawn on the water when the full moon is going down. To see the gathering dusk drink down the purple wine that dyes the air, the sea and the light clouds, until it is almost dark, and then to feel the darkness growing light again with the warm, yellow moon - to watch the jewels gathering on the velvet sea, and the sharp black cliffs turning to chiselled silver above you - to know that the whole night is to be but a softer day - to see how the love of the sun for the earth is one, and the love of the moon another - that is a moment for which one may give much and not be disappointed.

Beatrice Granmichele saw and felt what she had never seen or felt before, and the magic of Tragara held sway over her, as it does over the few who see it as she saw it. She turned slowly and glanced at San Miniato's face. The moonlight improved it, she thought. There seemed to be more vigour in the well-drawn lines, more strength in the forehead than she had noticed until now. She felt that she was in sympathy with him, and that the sympathy might be a lasting one. Then she turned quite round and faced the commonplace lamp with its pink shade, which stood on the dinner-table, and she experienced a disagreeable sensation. The Marchesa was slowly fanning herself, already seated at her place.

"If you are human beings, and not astronomers," she said, "we might perhaps dine."

"I am very human, for my part," said San Miniato, holding Beatrice's chair for her to sit down.

"There was really no use for the lamp, mamma," she said,

turning again to look at the moon. "You see what an illumination we have! San Miniato has provided us with something better than a lamp."

"San Miniato, my dear child, is a man of the highest genius. I always said so. But if you begin to talk of eating without a lamp, you may as well talk of abolishing civilisation."

"I wish we could!" exclaimed Beatrice.

"And so do I, with all my heart," said San Miniato.

"Including baccarat and quinze?" enquired the Marchesa, lazily picking out the most delicate morsels from the cold fish on her plate.

"Including baccarat, quinze, the world, the flesh and the devil," said San Miniato.

"Pray remember, dearest friend, that Beatrice is at the table," observed the Marchesa, with indolent reproach in her voice.

"I do," replied San Miniato. "It is precisely for her sake that I would like to do away with the things I have named."

"You might just leave a little of each for Sundays!" suggested the young girl.

"Beatrice!" exclaimed her mother.

CHAPTER VI

While the little party sat at table, the sailors gathered together at a distance among the rocks, and presently the strong red light of their fire shot up through the shadows, lending new contrasts to the scene. And there they slung their kettle on an oar and patiently waited for the water to boil, while the man known as the Gull, always cook in every crew in which he chanced to find himself, sat with the salt on one side of him and a big bundle of macaroni on the other, prepared to begin operations at any moment.

Ruggiero stood a little apart, his back against a boulder, his arms crossed and his eyes fixed on Beatrice's face. His keen sight could distinguish the changing play of her expression as readily at that distance as though he had been standing beside her, and he tried to catch the words she spoke, listening with a sort of hurt envy to the little silvery laugh that now and then echoed across the open space and lost itself in the crannies of the rocks. It all hurt him, and yet for nothing in the world would he have turned away or shut his ears. More than once, too, the thoughts that had disturbed him while he was steering in the afternoon, came upon him with renewed and startling strength. He had in him some of that red old blood that does not stop for trifles such as life and death when the hour of passion burns, and the brain reels with overmastering love.

And Bastianello was not in a much better case, though his was less hard to bear. The pretty Teresina had seated herself on a smooth rock in the moonlight, not far from the table, and as the dishes came back, the young sailor waited on her and served her with unrelaxed attention. Since Ruggiero would not take advantage of the situation, his brother saw no reason for not at least enjoying the pleasure of seeing the adorable Teresina eat and drink as it were from his hand. Why Ruggiero was so cold, and stood there against his rock, silent and glowering, Bastianello could not at all understand; nor had he any thought of taking an unfair advantage. Ruggiero was first and no one should interfere with him, or his love; but Bastianello, judging from what he felt himself, fancied that she might have given him some good advice. Teresina's cheeks flushed with pleasure and her eyes sparkled each time he brought her some dainty from the master's table, and she thanked him in the prettiest way imaginable, so that her voice reminded him of the singing of the yellow-beaked blackbird he kept in a cage at home - which was saying much, for the blackbird sang well and sweetly. But Bastianello only said each time that "it was nothing," and then stood silently waiting beside her till she should finish what she was eating and be ready for more. Teresina would doubtless have enjoyed a little conversation, and she looked up from time to time at the handsome sailor beside her, with a look of enquiry in her eyes, as though to ask why he said nothing. But Bastianello felt that he was on his honour, for he never doubted that the little maid was the cause of Ruggiero's disease of the heart and indeed of all that his brother evidently suffered, and he was too modest by nature to think that Teresina could prefer him to Ruggiero, who had always been the object of his own unbounded devotion and admiration. Presently, when there was nothing more to offer her, and the party at the table were lighting their cigarettes over their coffee, he went away and going up to Ruggiero drew him a little further aside from the group of sailors.

"I want to tell you something," he began. "You must not be as you are, a man like you."

"How may that be?" asked Ruggiero, still looking towards the table, and not pleased at being dragged from his former post of observation.

"I will tell you. I have been serving her with food. You could have done that instead if you had wished. You could have talked to her, and she would have liked it. It is easy when a woman is sitting apart and a man brings her good food and wine - you could have spoken a word into her ear."

Ruggiero was silent, but he slowly nodded twice, then shook his head.

"You do not say anything," continued Bastianello, "and you do wrong. What I tell you is true, and you cannot deny it. After all, we are men and they are women. Are they to speak first?"

"It is just," answered Ruggiero laconically.

"But then, per Dio, go and talk to her. Are you going to begin giving her the gold before you have spoken?"

From which question it will be clear to the unsophisticated foreigner that a regular series of presents in jewelry is the natural accompaniment of a well-to-do courtship in the south. The trinkets are called collectively "the gold."

Ruggiero did not find a ready answer to so strong an argument. Little guessing that his brother was almost as much in love with Teresina as he himself was with her mistress, he saw no reason for undeceiving him concerning his own feelings. Since Bastianello had discovered that he, Ruggiero, was suffering from an acute attack of the affections, it had become the latter's chief object to conceal the real truth. It was not so much, that he dreaded the ridicule - he, a poor sailor - of being known to love a great lady's daughter; ridicule was not among the things he feared. But something far too subtle for him to define made him keep his secret to himself - an inborn, chivalrous, manly instinct, inherited through generations of peasants but surviving still, as the trace of gold in the ashes of a rich stuff that has had gilded threads in it.

"If I did begin with the gold," he said at last, "and if she would not have me when I spoke afterwards, she would give the gold back."

"Of course she would. What do you take her for?" Bastianello asked the question almost angrily, for he loved Teresina and he resented the slightest imputation upon her fair dealing.

Ruggiero looked at him curiously, but was far too much preoccupied with his own thoughts to guess what the matter was. He turned away and went towards the fire where the Gull was already tasting a slippery string of the macaroni to find out whether it were enough cooked. Bastianello shrugged his shoulders and followed him in silence. Before long they were all seated round the huge earthen dish, each armed with an iron fork in one hand and a ship biscuit in the other, with which to catch the drippings neatly, according to good manners, in conveying the full fork from the dish to the wide-opened mouth. By and by there was a sound of liquid gurgling from a demijohn as it was poured into the big jug, and the wine went round quickly from hand to hand, while those who waited for their turn munched their biscuits. Some one has said that great appetites, like great passions, are silent. Hardly a word was said until the wine was passed a second time with a ration of hard cheese and another biscuit. Then the tongues were unloosed and the strange, uncouth jests of the rough men circulated in an undertone, and now and then one of them suffered agonies in smothering a huge laugh, lest his mirth should disturb the "excellencies" at their table. The latter, however, were otherwise engaged and paid little attention to the sailors.

The Marchesa di Mola, having eaten about six mouthfuls of twice that number of delicacies and having swallowed half a glass of champagne and a cup of coffee, was extended in her cane rocking-chair, with her back to the moon and her face to the lamp, trying to imagine herself in her comfortable sitting room at the hotel, or even in her own luxurious boudoir in her Sicilian home. The attempt was fairly successful, and the result was a passing taste of that self-satisfied beatitude which is the peculiar and enviable lot of very lazy people after dinner. She cared for nothing and she cared for nobody. San Miniato and Beatrice might sit over there by the water's edge, in the moonlight, and talk in low tones as long as they pleased. There were no tiresome people from the hotel to watch their proceedings, and nothing better could happen than that they should fall in love, be engaged and married forthwith. That was certainly not the way the Marchesa could have wished the courtship and marriage to develop and come to maturity, if there had been witnesses of the facts from amongst her near acquaintance. But since there was nobody to see, and since it was quite impossible that she should run after the pair when they chose to leave her side, resignation was the best policy, resignation without effort, without fatigue and without qualms. Moreover, San Miniato himself had told her that in some of the best families in the north of Italy it was considered permissible for a man to offer himself directly to a young lady, and San Miniato was undoubtedly familiar with the usages of the very best society. It was quite safe to trust to him.

San Miniato himself would have greatly preferred to leave the negotiations in the hands of the Marchesa and would have done so had he not known that she possessed no power whatever over Beatrice. But he saw that the Marchesa, however much she might desire the marriage, would never exert herself to influence her daughter. She was far too indolent, and at heart, perhaps, too indifferent, and she knew the value of money and especially of her own. San Miniato made up his mind that if he won at all, it must be upon his own merits and by his own efforts.

He had not found it hard to lead Beatrice away from the lamp when dinner was over, and after walking about on the rocks for a few minutes he proposed that they should sit down near the water, facing the moonlit sea. Beatrice sat upon a smooth projection and San Miniato placed himself at her feet, in such a position that he could look up into her face and talk to her without raising his voice.

"So you are glad you came here, Donna Beatrice," he said.

"Very glad," she answered. "It is something I have never seen before - something I shall never forget, as long as I live."

"Nor I."

"Have you a good memory?"

"For some things, not for others."

"For what, for instance?"

"For those I love -"

"And a bad memory for those whom you have loved," suggested Beatrice with a smile.

"Have you any reason for saying that?" asked San Miniato gravely. "You know too little of me and my life to judge of either. I have not loved many, and I have remembered them well."

"How many? A dozen, more or less? Or twenty? Or a hundred?"

"Two. One is dead, and one has forgotten me."

Beatrice was silent. It was admirably done, and for the first time he made her believe that he was in earnest. It had not been very hard for him either, for there was a foundation of truth in what he said. He had not always been a man without heart.

"It is much to have loved twice," said the young girl at last, in a dreamy voice. She was thinking of what had passed through her mind that afternoon.

"It is much - but not enough. What has never been lived out, is never enough."

"Perhaps - but who could love three times?"

"Any man - and the third might be the best and the strongest, as well as the last."

"To me it seems impossible."

San Miniato had got his chance and he knew it. He was nervous and not sure of himself, for he knew very well that she had but a passing attraction for him, beyond the very solid inducement to marry her offered by her fortune. But he knew that the opportunity must not be lost, and he did not waste time. He spoke quietly, not wishing to risk a dramatic effect until he could count on his own rather slight histrionic powers.

"So it seems impossible to you, Donna Beatrice," he said, in a musing tone. "Well, I daresay it does. Many things must seem impossible to you which are rather startling facts to me. I am older than you, I am a man, and I have been a soldier. I have lived a life such as you cannot dream of - not worse perhaps than that of many another man, but certainly not better. And I am quite sure that if I gave you my history you would not understand four-fifths of it, and the other fifth would shock you. Of course it would - how could it be otherwise? How could you and I look at anything from quite the same point of view?"

"And yet we often agree," said Beatrice, thoughtfully.

"Yes, we do. That is quite true. And that is because a certain sympathy exists between us. I feel that very much when I am with you, and that is one reason why I try to be with you as much as possible."

"You say that is one reason. Have you many others?" Beatrice tried to laugh a little, but she felt somehow that laughter was out of place and that a serious moment in her life had come at last, in which it would be wiser to be grave and to think well of what she was doing.

"One chief one, and many little ones," answered San Miniato. "You are good to me, you are young, you are fresh - you are gifted and unlike the others, and you have a rare charm such as I never met in any woman. Are those not all good reasons? Are they not enough?"

"If they were all true, they would be more than enough. Is the chief reason the last?"

"It is the last of all. I have not given it to you yet. Some things are better not said at all."

"They must be bad things," answered Beatrice, with an air of innocence.

She was beginning to understand, at last, that he really intended to make her a declaration of love. It was unheard of, almost inconceivable. But there he was at her feet, looking very handsome in the moonlight, his face turned up to hers with an unmistakable look of devotion in its rather grave lines. His voice, too, had a new sound in it. Indifferent as he might be by daylight and in ordinary life, the magic of the place and scene affected him a little at the present moment. Perhaps a memory of other years, when his pulse had quickened and his voice had trembled oddly, just touched his heart now and it responded with a faint thrill. For a moment at least he forgot his sordid plan, and Beatrice's own personal attraction was upon him.

And she was very lovely as she sat there, looking down at him, with white folded hands, hatless in the warm night, her eyes full of the dancing rays that trembled upon the softly rippling water.

"If they are not bad things," she said, speaking again, "why do you not tell them to me?"

"You would laugh."

"I have laughed enough to-night. Tell me!"

"Tell you! Yes - that is easy to do. But it would be so hard to make you understand! It is the difference between a word and a thought, between belief and mere show, between truth and hearsay - more than that - much more than I can tell you. It means so much to me - it may mean so little to you, when I have said it!"

"But if you do not say it, how can I guess it, or try to understand it?"

"Would you try? Would you?"

"Yes."

Her voice was soft, gentle, persuasive. She felt something she had never felt, and it must be love, she thought. She had always liked him a little better than the rest. But surely, this was more than mere liking. She had a strange longing to hear him say the words, to start, as her instinct told her she must, when he spoke them, to be told for the first time that she was loved. Is it strange, after all? Young, imaginative and full of life, she had been brought up to believe that she was to be married to some man she scarcely knew, after a week's acquaintance, without so much as having talked five minutes with him alone; she had been taught that love was a legend and matrimony a matter of interest. And yet here was the man whom her mother undoubtedly wished her to marry, not only talking with her as they had often talked before, with no one to hear what was said, but actually on the verge of telling her that he loved her. Could anything be more delicious, more original, more in harmony with the place and hour? And as if all this were not enough, she really felt the touch and thrill of love in her own heart, and the leaping wonder to know what was to come.

F. Marion Crawford

She had told him to speak and she waited for his voice. He, on his part, knew that much was at stake, for he saw that she was moved, and that all depended on his words. The fewer the better, he thought, if only there could be a note of passion in them, if only one of them could ring as all of poor Ruggiero's had rung when he had spoken that afternoon. He hesitated and hesitation would be fatal if it lasted another five seconds. He grew desperate. Where were the words and the tone that had broken down the will of other women, far harder to please than this mere child? He felt everything at once, except love. He saw her fortune slipping from him at the very moment of getting it, he felt a little contempt for the part he was playing and a sovereign scorn for his own imbecility, he even anticipated the Marchesa's languid but cutting comments on his failure. One second more, and all was lost - but not a word would come. Then, in sheer despair and with a violence that betrayed it, he seized one of Beatrice's hands in both of his and kissed it madly a score of times. As she interpreted the action, no eloquence of words could have told her more of what she wished to hear. It was unexpected, it was passionate; if it had been premeditated, it would have been a stroke of genius. As it was, it was a stroke of luck for San Miniato. With the true gambler's instinct he saw that he was winning and his hesitation disappeared. His voice trembled passionately now with excitement, if not with love - but it was the same to Beatrice, who heard the quick-spoken words that followed, and drank them in as a thirsty man swallows the first draught of wine he can lay hands on, be it ever so acid.

At the first moment she had been startled and had almost uttered a short cry, half of delight and half of fear. But she had no wish to alarm her mother and the quick thought stifled her voice. She tried to withdraw her hand, but he held it tightly in his own which were cold as ice, and she sat still listening to all he said.

"Ah, Beatrice!" he was saying, "you have given me back life itself! Can you guess what I have lived through in these days? Can you imagine how I have thought of you and suffered day and night, and said to myself that I should never have your love? Can you dream what it must be to a man like me, lonely, friendless, half heart-broken, to find the one jewel worth living for, the one light worth seeking, the one woman worth loving - and then to long for her almost without hope, and so long? It is long, too. Who counts the days or the weeks when he loves? It is as though we had loved from the beginning of our lives! Can you or I imagine what it all was like before we met? I cannot remember that past time. I had no life before it - it is all forgotten, all gone, all buried and for ever. You have made everything new to me, new and beautiful and full of light - ah, Beatrice! How I love you!"

Rather a long speech at such a moment, an older woman would have thought, and not over original in choice of similes and epithets, but fluent enough and good enough to serve the purpose and to turn the current of Beatrice's girlish life. Yet not much of a love-speech. Ruggiero's had been better, as a little true steel is better than much iron at certain moments in life. It succeeded very well at the moment, but its ultimate success would have been surer if it had reached no ears but Beatrice's. Neither she nor San Miniato were aware that a few feet below them a man was lying on his back, with white face and clenched hands, staring at the pale moonlit sky above him, and listening in stony despair to every word that was spoken.

The sight would have disturbed them, had they seen it, though they both were fearless by nature and not easily startled. Had Beatrice seen Ruggiero at that moment, she would have learned once and for ever the difference between real passion and its counterfeit. But Ruggiero knew where he was and had no intention of betraying himself by voice or movement. He suffered almost all that a man can suffer by the heart alone, but he was strong and could bear torture.

The hardest of all was that he understood the real truth, partly by instinct and partly through what he knew of his master. Those rough southern sailors sometimes have a wonderful keenness in discovering the meaning of their masters' doings.

Ruggiero held the key to the situation. He knew that San Miniato was poor and that the Marchesa was very rich. He knew very well that San Miniato was not at all in love, for he knew what love really meant, and he could see how the Count always acted by calculation and never from impulse. Best of all he saw that Beatrice was a mere child who was being deceived by the coolly assumed passion of a veteran woman-killer. It was bitterly hard to bear. And he had felt a foreboding of it all in the afternoon - and he wished that he had risked all and brought down the brass tiller on San Miniato's head and submitted to be sent to the galleys for life. He could never have forgotten Beatrice; but San Miniato could never have married her, and that satisfaction would have made chains light and hard labour a pastime.

It was too late to think of such things now. Had he yielded to the first murderous impulse, it would have been better. But he had never struck a man from behind and he knew that he could not do it in cold blood. Yet how much better it would have been! He would not be lying now on the rock, holding his breath and clenching his fists, listening to his Excellency the Count of San Miniato's love making. By this time the Count of San Miniato would be cold, and he, Ruggiero, would be handcuffed and locked up in the little barrack of the gendarmes at Sorrento, and Beatrice with her mother would be recovering from their fright as best they could in the rooms at the hotel, and Teresina would be crying, and Bastianello would be sitting at the door of his brother's prison waiting to see what happened and ready to do what he could. Truly all this would have been much better! But the moment had passed and he must lie on his rock in silence, bound hand and foot by the necessity of hiding himself, and giving his heart to be torn to pieces by San Miniato's aristocratic fine gentleman's hands, and burned through and through by Beatrice's gentle words.

"And so you really love me?" said San Miniato, sure at last of his victory.

"Do you doubt it, after what I have done?" asked Beatrice in a very soft voice. "Did I not leave my hand in yours when you took it so roughly and - you know -"

"When I kissed it - but I want the words, too - only once, from your beautiful lips -"

"The words -" Beatrice hesitated. They were too new to her lips, and a soft blush rose in her cheeks, visible even in the moonlight.

Ruggiero's heart stood still - not for the first time that day. Would she speak the three syllables or not?

As for San Miniato, his excitement had cooled, and he threw all the tenderness he could muster into, his last request, with instinctive tact returning to the more quiet tone he had used at the beginning of the conversation.

"I ask you, Beatrice mia, to say -" he paused, to give the proper effect in the right place - "I love you," he said, completing the sentence very musically and looking up most tenderly into her eyes.

She sighed, blushed again, and turned her head away. Then quite suddenly she looked at him once more, pressed his hand nervously and spoke.

"I love you, carissimo," she said, and rose at the same moment from her seat. "Come - it is time. Mamma will be tired," she added, while he held her hand and pressed it to his lips.

Her confusion had made it easy for him. He would have had difficulty in ending the scene artistically if she had not unconsciously helped him.

Ruggiero clenched his hands a little tighter and tried not to breathe.

"It is a lie," he said in his heart, but his lips never moved, nor did he stir a limb as he listened to the departing footsteps on the ledge above.

Then with the ease of great strength he drew himself along through cranny and hollow till he was far from where they sat, and had reached the place where the boats were made fast. It would seem natural to every one that he should suddenly be standing there to see that all was right, and that none of the moorings had slipped or chafed against the jagged rocks. There he stood, gazing at the rippling water, at the tall yards as they slowly crossed and recrossed the face of the moon, with the rocking of the boats, at the cliffs to the right and left, at the dim headland of the Campanella, at all the sights long familiar to him - seeing none of them and yet feeling that they at least were his own people, that they understood him and knew what he felt - what he had no words with which to tell any one, if he had wished to tell it.

For he who loves and is little loved, or not at all, has no friend, be he of high estate or low, beyond nature, the deep-bosomed, the bountiful, the true; and on her he may lean, trusting, and know that he will not be betrayed. And in time her language will be his. But she will be heard alone when she speaks with him, and without rival, with the full right of a woman who gives all her love and asks for a man's soul in return, recking little of all the world besides. But not all know how kind she is, how merciful and how sweet. For she does not heal broken hearts. She takes them as they are into her own, with all the memory and all the sin, perhaps, and all the bitter sorrow which is the reward of faith and faithlessness alike. She takes them all, and holds them kindly in her own breast, as she has taken the torn limbs of martyred saints and tortured sinners and has softly turned them all into a fragrant dust. And though the ashes of the heart be very bitter, they are after all but dust, which cannot feel of itself any more. Yet there may be something left behind, in the place where it lived and was broken and died, which is not wholly bad, though there be little good in this earth where there is no heart.

Moreover, nature is a silent mistress to all but those who love her, and she tells no tales as men and women do, and forgets none of the secrets which are told to her, for they are our treasures - treasures of love and of hate, of sweetness and of poison, which we lay up in her keeping when we are alone with her, sure that we shall find again all we have given up if we require it of her. But as the years blossom, bloom, and fade in their quick succession, the day will come when we shall ask of her only the balm and be glad to leave the poison hidden, and to forget how we would have used it in old days - when we shall ask her only to give us the memory of a dear and gentle hand - dear still but no longer kind - of the voice that was once a harmony, and whose harsh discord is almost music still - of the hour when love was twofold, stainless and supreme. Those things we shall ask of her and she, in her wonderful tenderness, will give them to us again - in dreams, waking or sleeping, in the sunlit silence of lonely places, in soft nights when the southern sea is still, in the greater loneliness of the storm, when brave faces are set as stone and freezing hands grasp frozen ropes, and the shadow of death rises from the waves and stands between every man and his fellows. We shall ask, and we shall receive. Out of noon-day shadow, out of the starlit dusk, out of the driving spray of the midtempest, one face will rise, one hand will touch our own, one loving, lingering glance will meet ours from eyes that have no look of love for us in them now. These things our lady nature will give us of all those we have given her. But of the others, we shall not ask for them, and she will mercifully forget for us the bitterness of their birth, and life, and death.

CHAPTER VII

"I THOUGHT I was never to see you again," observed the Marchesa, as Beatrice and San Miniato came to her side.

"Judging from your calm, you were bearing the separation with admirable fortitude," answered the Count.

"Dearest friend, one has to bear so much in this life!"

Beatrice stood beside the table, resting one hand upon it and looking back towards the place where she had been sitting. San Miniato took the Marchesa's hand and raised it to his lips, pressed it a little and then nodded slowly, with a significant look. The Marchesa's sleepy eyes opened suddenly with an expression of startled satisfaction, and she returned the pressure of the fingers with more energy than San Miniato had suspected. She was evidently very much pleased. Perhaps the greatest satisfaction of all was the certainty that she was to have no more trouble in the matter, since it had been undertaken, negotiated and settled by the principals between them. Then she raised her eyebrows and moved her head a little as though to inquire what had taken place, but San Miniato made her understand by a sign that he could not speak before Beatrice.

"Beatrice, my angel," said the Marchesa, with more than usual sweetness, "you have sat so long upon that rock that you have almost reconciled me to Tragara. Do you not think that you could go back and sit there five minutes longer?"

Beatrice glanced quickly at her mother and then at San Miniato and turned away without a word, leaving the two together.

"And now, San Miniato carissimo," said the Marchesa, "sit down beside me on that chair, and tell me what has happened, though I think I already understand. You have spoken to Beatrice?"

"I have spoken - yes - and the result is favourable. I am the happiest of men."

"Do you mean to say that she answered you at once?" asked the Marchesa, affecting, as usual, to be scandalised.

"She answered me - yes, dear Marchesa - she told me that she loved me. It only remains for me to claim the maternal blessing which you so generously promised in advance."

Somehow it was a relief to him to return to the rather stiff and over-formal phraseology which he always used on important occasions when speaking to her, and which, as he well knew, flattered her desire to be thought a very great lady.

"As for my blessing, you shall have it, and at once. But indeed, I am most curious to know exactly what she said, and what you said - I, who am never curious about anything!"

"Two words tell the story. I told her I loved her and she answered that she loved me."

"Dearest friend, how long it took you to say those two words! You must have hesitated a good deal."

"To tell the truth, there was more said than that. I will not deny the grave imputation. I spoke of my past life -"

"Dio mio! To my daughter! How could you -" The Marchesa raised her hands and let them fall again.

"But why not?" asked San Miniato, suppressing a smile. "Have I been such an impossibly bad man that the very mention of my past must shock a young girl - whom I love?" In the last words he found an opportunity to practise the expression of a little passion, and took advantage of it, well knowing that it would be useful in the immediate future.

"I never said that!" protested the Marchesa. "But we all know something about you, dear Don Juan!"

"Calumnies, nothing but calumnies!"

"But such pretty calumnies - you might almost accept them. I should think none the worse of you if they were all true."

"You are charming, dearest Marchesa. I kiss your generous hand! As a matter of fact, I only told Donna Beatrice - may I call her Beatrice to you now, as I have long called her in my heart? I only told her that I had been unhappy, that I had loved twice - once a woman who is dead, once another who has long ago forgotten me. That was all. Was it so very bad? Her heart was softened - she is so gentle! And then I told her that a greater and stronger passion than those now filled my present life, and last of all I told her that I loved her."

"And she returned the compliment immediately?" asked the Marchesa, slowly selecting a sugared chestnut from the plate beside her, turning it round, examining it and at last putting it into her mouth.

"How lightly you speak of what concerns life and death!" sighed San Miniato. "No - Beatrice did not answer immediately. I said much more - far more than I can remember. How can you ask me to repeat word for word the unpremeditated outpourings of a happy passion? The flood has swept by, leaving deep traces - but who can remember where the eddies and rapids were?"

"You are very poetical, caro mio. Your language delights me -

it is the language of the heart. Pray give me one of those little cigarettes you smoke. Yes - and a light - and now the least drop of champagne. I will drink your health."

"And I both yours and Beatrice's," answered San Miniato, filling his own glass.

"You may put Beatrice first, since she is yours."

"But without you there would be no Beatrice, gentilissima," said the Count gallantly, when he had emptied his glass.

"That is true, and pretty besides. And so," continued the Marchesa in a tone of languid reflection, "you have actually been making love to my daughter, beyond my hearing, alone on the rocks - and I gave you my permission, and now you are engaged to be married! It is too extraordinary to be believed. That was not the way I was married. There was more formality in those days."

Indeed, she could not imagine the deceased Granmichele throwing himself upon his knees at her feet, even upon the softest of carpets.

"Then I thank the fates that those days are over!" returned San Miniato.

"Perhaps I should, too. I am not sure that the conclusion would have been so satisfactory, if I had undertaken to persuade Beatrice. She is headstrong and capricious, and so painfully energetic! Every discussion with her shortens my life by a year."

"She is an angel in her caprice," answered the Count with conviction. "Indeed, much of her charm lies in her changing moods."

"If she is an angel, what am I?" asked the Marchesa. "Such a contrast!"

"She is the angel of motion - you are the angel of repose."

"You are delightful to-night."

While this conversation was taking place, Beatrice had wandered away over the rocks alone, not heeding the unevenness of the stones and taking little notice of the direction of her walk. She only knew that she would not go back to the place where she had sat, not for all the world. A change had taken place already and she was angry with herself for what she had done in all sincerity.

She was hurt and her first illusion had suffered a grave shock almost at the moment of its birth. She asked herself how it could be possible, if San Miniato loved her as he had said he did, that he should not feel as she felt and understand love as she did - as something secret and sacred, to be kept from other eyes. Her instinct told her easily enough that San Miniato was at that very moment telling her mother all that had taken place, and she bitterly resented the thought. It would surely have been enough, if he had waited until the following day and then formally asked her hand of the Marchesa. It would have been better, more natural in every way, just now when they had gone up to the table, if he had said simply that they loved one another and had asked her mother's blessing. Anything rather than to feel that he was coolly describing the details of the first love scene in her life - the thousandth, perhaps, in his own.

After all, did she love him? Did he really love her? His passionate manner when he had seized her hand had moved her strangely, and she had listened with a sort of girlish wonder to his declarations of devotion afterwards. But now, in the, calm moonlight and quite alone, she could hear Ruggiero's deep strong voice in her ears, and the few manly words he had uttered. There was not much in them in the way of eloquence - a sailor's picturesque phrase - she had heard something like it before. But there had been strength, and the power to do, and the will to act in every intonation of his speech. She remembered every word San Miniato had spoken, far better than he would remember it himself in a day or two, and she was ready to analyse and criticise now what had charmed and pleased her a moment earlier. Why was he going over it all to her mother, like a lesson learnt and repeated? She was so glad to be alone - she would have been so glad to think alone of what she had taken for the most delicious moment of her young life. If he were really in earnest, he would feel as she did and would have said at once that it was late and time to be going home - he would have invented any excuse to escape the interview which her mother would try to force upon him. Could it be love that he felt? And if not, as her heart told her it was not, what was his object in playing such a comedy? She knew well enough, from Teresina, that many a young Neapolitan nobleman would have given his title for her fortune, but Teresina, perhaps for reasons of her own, never dared to cast such an aspersion upon San Miniato, even in the intimate conversation which sometimes takes place between an Italian lady and her maid - and, indeed, if the truth be told, between maids and their mistresses in most parts of the world.

But the doubt thrust itself forward now. Beatrice was quick to doubt at all times. She was also capricious and changeable about matters which did not affect her deeply, and those that did were few enough. It was certainly possible that San Miniato, after all, only wanted her money and that her mother was willing to give it in return for a great name and a great position. She felt that if the case had been stated to her from the first in its true light she might have accepted the situation without illusion, but without disgust. Everybody, her mother said, was married by arrangement, some for one advantage, some for the sake of another. After all, San Miniato was better than most of the rest. There was a certain superiority about him which she would like to see in her husband, a certain simple elegance, a certain outward dignity, which pleased her. But when her mother had spoken in her languid way of the marriage, Beatrice had resented the denial of her free will, and had answered that she would please herself or not marry at all. The Marchesa, far too lacking in energy to sustain such a contest, had contented herself with her favourite expression of horror at her daughter's unfilial conduct. Now, however, Beatrice felt that if it had all been arranged for her, she would have been satisfied, but that since San Miniato had played something very like a comedy, she would refuse to be duped by it. She was very bitter against him in the first revulsion of feeling and treated him more hardly in her thoughts than he, perhaps, deserved.

And there he was, up there by the table, telling her mother of his success. Her blood rose in her cheeks at the thought and she stamped her foot upon the rock out of sheer anger at herself, at him, at everything and everybody. Then she moved on.

Ruggiero was standing at the edge of the water looking out to sea. The moonlight silvered his white face and fair beard and accentuated the sharp black line where his sailor's cap crossed his forehead. Wild and angry emotions chased each other from his heart to his brain and back again, firing his overwrought nerves and heated blood, as the flame runs along a train of powder. He heard a light step behind him and turned suddenly. Beatrice was close upon him.

"Is that you, Ruggiero," she asked, for she had seen him with his back turned and had not recognised him at first.

"Yes, Excellency," he answered in a hoarse voice, touching his cap.

"What a beautiful night it is!" said the young girl. She often talked with the men in the boat, and Ruggiero interested her especially at the present moment.

"Yes, Excellency," he answered again.

"Is the weather to be fine, Ruggiero?"

"Yes, Excellency."

Ruggiero was apparently not in the conversational mood. He was probably thinking of the girl he loved - in all likelihood of Teresina, as Beatrice thought. She stood still a couple of paces from him and looked at the sea. She felt a capricious desire to make the big sailor talk and tell her something about himself. It would be sure to be interesting and honest and strong, a contrast, as she fancied, to the things she had just heard.

"Ruggiero -" she began, and then she stopped and hesitated.

"Yes, Excellency."

The continual repetition of the two words irritated her. She tried to frame a question to which he could not give the same answer.

"I would like you to tell me who it is whom you love so dearly - is she good and beautiful and sensible, too, as you said?"

"She is all that, Excellency." His voice shook, not as it seemed to her with weakness, but with strength.

"Tell me her name."

Ruggiero was silent for some moments, and his head was bent forward. He seemed to be breathing hard and not able to speak.

"Her name is Beatrice," he said at last, in a low, firm tone as though he were making a great effort.

"Really!" exclaimed the young girl. "That is my name, too. I suppose that is why you did not want to tell me. But you must not be afraid of me, Ruggiero. If there is anything I can do to help you, I will do it. Is it money you need? I will give you some."

"It is not money."

"What is it, then?"

"Love - and a miracle."

His answers came lower and lower, and he looked at the ground, suffering as he had never suffered and yet indescribably happy in speaking with her, and in seeing the interest she felt in him. But his brain was beginning to reel. He did not know what he might say next.

"Love and a miracle!" repeated Beatrice in her silvery voice. "Those are two things which I cannot get for you. You must pray to the saints for the one and to her for the other. Does she not love you at all then?"

"She will never love me. I know it."

"And that would be the miracle - if she ever should? Such miracles have been done by men themselves without the help of the saints, before now."

Ruggiero looked up sharply and he felt his hands shaking. He thought she was speaking of what had just happened, of which he had been a witness.

"Such miracles as that may happen - but they are the devil's miracles."

Beatrice was silent for a moment. She was indeed inclined to believe in a special intervention of the powers of evil in her own case. Had she not been suddenly moved to tell a man that she loved him, only to discover a moment later that it was a mistake?

"What is the miracle you pray for, Ruggiero?" she asked after a pause.

"To be changed into some one else, Excellency."

"And then - would she love you?"

"By Our Lady's grace - perhaps!" The deep voice shook again. He set his teeth, folded his arms over his throbbing breast, and planted one foot firmly on a stone before him, as though to await a blow.

"I am very sorry for you, Ruggiero," said Beatrice in soft, kind tones.

"God render you your kindness - it is better than nothing," he answered.

"Is she sorry for you, too? She should be - you love her so much."

"Yes - she is sorry for me. She has just said so." He raised his clenched hand to his mouth almost before the words were uttered. Beatrice did not see the few bright red drops that fell upon the rock as he gnawed the flesh.

"Just said so?" she said, repeating his words. "I do not understand? Is she here to-night?"

He did not answer, but slowly bent his head, as though in assent. An odd foreboding of danger shot through the young girl's heart. Little as the man said, he seemed desperate. It was possible that the girl he loved might be a Capriote, and that he might have met her and talked with her while the dinner was going on. He might have strangled her with those great hands of his. She would not have uttered a cry, and no one would be the wiser, for Tragara is a lonely place, by day and night.

"She is here, you say?" Beatrice asked again. "Where is she? Ruggiero, what is the matter? Have you done her any harm? Have you hurt her? Have you killed her?"

"Not yet -"

"Not yet!" Beatrice cried, in a low horror-struck tone. She had heard his sharp, agonised breathing as he reeled unsteadily against the rock behind him. She was a rarely courageous girl. Instead of shrinking she made a step forward and took him firmly by the arm.

"What have you done, Ruggiero?" she asked sternly.

He felt that she was accusing him. His face grew ashy white, and grave - almost grand, she thought afterwards, for she remembered long the look he wore. His answer came slowly in deep, vibrating tones.

"I have done nothing - but love her."

"Show her to me - take me to her," said Beatrice, still dreading some horrible deed, she scarcely knew why.

"She is here."

"Where?"

"Here! - Ah, Christ."

His great hands went out madly as though to take her, then tenderly touched the loose sleeves she wore, then fell, as though lifeless, to his sides again.

Beatrice passed her hand over her eyes and drew back quickly a step. She was startled and angered, but not frightened. It was almost the repetition of the waking dream that had flitted through her brain before she had landed. She had heard the grand ring of passionate love this once at least - and how? In the voice of a common sailor - out of the heart of an ignorant fellow who could neither read nor write, nor speak his own language, a churl, a peasant's son, a labourer - but a man, at least. That was it - a strong, honest, fearless man. That was why it all moved her so - that was why it was not an insult that this low-born fellow should dare to tell her he loved her. She opened her lids again and saw his great figure leaning back against the rock, his white face turned upward, his eyes half closed. She went near to him again. Instantly, he made an effort and stood upright. Her instinct told her that he wanted neither pity nor forgiveness nor comfort.

"You are a brave, strong man, Ruggiero; I will always pray that you may love some one who will love you again - since you can love so well."

The unspoiled girl's nature had found the right expression, and the only one. Ruggiero looked at her one moment, stooped and touched the hem of her white frock with two fingers and then pressed them silently to his lips. Who knows from what far age that outward act of submission and vassalage has been handed down in southern lands? There it is to this day, rarely seen, but still surviving and still known to all.

Then Ruggiero turned away and went up the sloping rocks again, and Beatrice stood still for a moment, watching his tall, retreating figure. She meant to go, too, but she lingered a while, knowing that if ever she came back to Tragara, this would be the spot where she would pause and recall a memory, and not that other, where she had sat while San Miniato played out his wretched little comedy.

It all rushed across her mind again, bringing a new sense of disgust and repulsion with it, and a new blush of shame and anger at having been so deceived. There was no doubt now. The contrast had been too great, too wide, too evident. It was the difference between truth and hearsay, as San Miniato had said once that night. There was no mistaking the one for the other.

Poor Ruggiero! that was why he was growing pale and thin. That was why his arm trembled when he helped her into the boat. She leaned against the rock and wondered what it all meant, whether there were really any justice in heaven or any happiness on earth. But she would not marry San Miniato, now, for she had given no promise. If she had done so, she would not have broken it - in that, at least, she was like other girls of her age and class. Next to evils of which she knew nothing, the breaking of a promise of marriage was the greatest and most unpardonable of sins, no matter what the circumstances might be. But she was sure that she had not promised anything.

At that moment in her meditations she heard the tread of a man's heel on the rocks. The sailors were all barefoot, and she knew it must be San Miniato. Unwilling to be alone with him even for a minute, she sprang lightly forward to meet him as he came. He held out his hand to help her, but she refused it by a gesture and hurried on.

"I have been speaking with your mother," he said, trying to take advantage of the thirty or forty yards that still remained to be traversed.

"So I suppose, as I left you together," she answered in a hard voice. "I have been talking to Ruggiero."

"Has anything displeased you, Beatrice?" asked San Miniato, surprised by her manner.

"No. Why do you call me Beatrice?" Her tone was colder than ever.

"I suppose I might be permitted -"

"You are not."

San Miniato looked at her in amazement, but they were already within earshot of the Marchesa, who had not moved from her long chair, and he did not risk anything more, not knowing what sort of answer he might get. But he was no novice, and as soon as he thought over the situation he remembered others similar to it in his experience, and he understood well enough that a sensitive young girl might feel ashamed of having shown too much feeling, or might have taken offence at some detail in his conduct which had entirely escaped his own notice. Young and vivacious women are peculiarly subject to this sort of sensitiveness, as he was well aware. There was nothing to be done but to be quiet, attentive in small things, and to wait for fair weather again. After all, he had crossed the Rubicon, and had been very well received on the other side. It would not be easy to make him go back again.

"My angel," said the Marchesa, throwing away the end of her cigarette, "you have caught cold. We must go home immediately."

"Yes, mamma."

With all her languor and laziness and selfishness, the Marchesa was not devoid of tact, least of all where her own ends were concerned, and when she took the trouble to have any object in life at all. She saw in her daughter's face that something had annoyed her, and she at once determined that no reference should be made to the great business of the moment, and that it would be best to end the evening in general conversation, leaving San Miniato no further opportunity of being alone with Beatrice. She guessed well enough that the girl was not really in love, but had yielded in a measure to the man's practised skill in love-making, but she was really anxious that the result should be permanent.

Beatrice was grateful to her for putting an end to the situation. The young girl was pale and her bright eyes had suddenly grown tired and heavy. She sat down beside her mother and shaded her brow against the lamp with her hand, while San Miniato went to give orders about returning.

"My dear child," said the Marchesa, "I am converted; it has been a delightful excursion; we have had an excellent dinner, and I am not at all tired. I am sure you have given yourself quite as much trouble about it as San Miniato."

Beatrice laughed nervously.

"There were a good many things to remember," she said, "but I wish there had been twice as many - it was so amusing to make out the list of all your little wants."

"What a good daughter you are to me, my angel," sighed the Marchesa.

It was not often that she showed so much, affection. Possibly she was rarely conscious of loving her child very much, and on the present occasion the emotion was not so overpowering as to have forced her to the expression of it, had she not seen the necessity for humouring the girl and restoring her normal good temper. On the whole, a very good understanding existed between the two, of such a nature that it would have been hard to destroy it. For it was impossible to quarrel with the Marchesa, for the simple reason that she never attempted to oppose her daughter, and rarely tried to oppose any one else. She was quite insensible to Beatrice's occasional reproaches concerning her indolence, and Beatrice had so much sense, in spite of her small caprices and whims, that it was always safe to let her have her own way. The consequence was that difficulties rarely arose between the two.

Beatrice smiled carelessly at the affectionate speech. She knew its exact value, but was not inclined to depreciate it in her own estimation. Just then she would rather have been left alone with her mother than with any one else, unless she could be left quite to herself.

"You are always very good to me, mamma," she answered; "you let me have my own way, and that is what I like best."

"Let you have it, carissima! You take it. But I am quite satisfied."

"After all, it saves you trouble," laughed Beatrice.

Just then San Miniato came back and was greatly relieved to see that Beatrice's usual expression had returned, and to hear her careless, tuneful laughter. In an incredibly short space of time the boat was ready, the Marchesa was lifted in her chair and carried to it, and all the party were aboard. The second boat, with its crew, was left to bring home the paraphernalia, and Ruggiero cast off the mooring and jumped upon the stern, as the men forward dipped their oars and began to pull out of the little sheltered bay.

There he sat again, perched in his old place behind his master, the latter's head close to his knee, holding the brass tiller in his hand. It would be hard to say what he felt, but it was not what he had felt before. It was all a dream, now, the past, the present and the future. He had told Beatrice - Donna Beatrice Granmichele, the fine lady - that he loved her, and she had not laughed in his face, nor insulted him, nor cried out for help. She had told him that he was brave and strong. Yet he knew that he had put forth all his strength and summoned all his courage in the great effort to be silent, and had failed. But that mattered little. He had got a hundred, a thousand times more kindness than he would have dared to hope for, if he had ever dared to think of saying what he had really said. He had been forced to what he had done, as a strong man is forced struggling against odds to the brink of a precipice, and he had found not death, but a strange new strength to live. He had not found Heaven, but he had touched the gates of Paradise and heard the sweet clear voice of the angel within. It was well for him that his hand had not been raised that afternoon to deal the one blow that would have decided his life. It was well that it was the summer time and that when he had put the helm down to go about there had been no white squall seething along with its wake of snowy foam from a quarter of a mile to windward. It would have been all over now and those great moments down there by the rocks would never have been lived.

"Through the arch, Ruggiero," said San Miniato to him as the boat cleared the rocks of the landward needle.

F. Marion Crawford

"Let us go home," said Beatrice, with a little impatience in her voice. "I am so tired."

Would she be tired of such a night if she loved the man beside her? Ruggiero thought not, any more than he would ever be weary of being near her to steer the boat that bore her - even for ever.

"It is so beautiful," said San Miniato.

Beatrice said nothing, but made an impatient movement that betrayed that she was displeased.

"Home, Ruggiero," said San Miniato's voice.

"Make sail!" Ruggiero called out, he himself hauling out the mizzen. A minute later the sails filled and the boat sped out over the smooth water, white-winged as a sea-bird under the great summer moon.

CHAPTER VIII

It was late on the following morning when the Marchesa came out upon her curtained terrace, moving slowly, her hands hanging listlessly down, her eyes half closed, as though regretting the sleep she might be still enjoying. Beatrice was sitting by a table, an open book beside her which she was not reading, and she hardly noticed her mother's light step. The young girl had spent a sleepless night, and for the first time since she had been a child a few tears had wet her pillow. She could not have told exactly why she had cried, for she had not felt anything like sadness, and tears were altogether foreign to her nature. But the unsought return of all the impressions of the evening had affected her strangely, and she felt all at once shame, anger and regret - shame at having been so easily deceived by the play of a man's face and voice, anger against him for the part he had acted, and regret for something unknown but dreamt of and almost understood, and which could never be. She was too young and girlish to understand that her eyes had been opened upon the workings of the human heart. She had seen two sights which neither man nor woman can ever forget, love and love's counterfeit presentment, and both were stamped indelibly upon the unspotted page of her maiden memory.

She had seen a man whom she had hitherto liked, and whom she had unconsciously respected for a certain dignity he seemed to have, degrade himself - and for money's sake, as she rightly judged - to the playing of a pitiful comedy. As the whole scene came back to her in all distinctness, she traced the deception from first to last with amazing certainty of comprehension, and she knew that San Miniato had wilfully and intentionally laid a plot to work upon her feelings and to produce the result he had obtained - a poor result enough, if he had known the whole truth, yet one of which Beatrice was sorely ashamed. She had been deceived into the expression of something which she had never felt - and which, this morning, seemed further from her than ever before. It was bitter to think that any man could say she had uttered those three words "I love you," when there was less truth in them than in the commonest, most pardonable social lie. He had planned the excursion, knowing how beautiful things in nature affected her, knowing exactly at what point the moon would rise, precisely at what hour that mysterious light would gleam upon the water, knowing the magic of the place and counting upon it to supplement his acting where it lacked reality. It had been clever of him to think it out so carefully, to plan each detail so thoughtfully, to behave so naturally until his opportunity was all prepared and ready for him. But for one little mistake, one moment's forgetfulness of tact, the impression might have remained and grown in distinctness until it would have secured the imprint of a strong reality at the beginning of a new volume in her life, to which she could always look back in the hereafter as to something true and sweet to be thought of. But his tact had failed him at the critical and supreme moment when he had got what he wanted and had not known how to keep it, even for an hour. And his mistake had been followed by a strange accident which had revealed to Beatrice the very core of a poor human heart that was beating itself to death, in true earnest, for her sake.

She had seen what many a woman longs for but may never look upon. She had seen a man, brave, strong, simple and true, with the death mark of his love for her upon his face. What matter if he were but an unlettered sailor, scarcely knowing what moved him nor the words he spoke? Beatrice was a woman and, womanlike, she knew without proof or testimony that his heart and hands were clean of the few sins which woman really despises in man.

They are not many - be it said in honour of womanly generosity and kindness - they are not many, those bad deeds which a woman cannot forgive, and that she is right is truly shown in that those are the sins which the most manly men despise in others. They are, I think, cowardice, lying for selfish ends, betraying tales of woman's weakness - almost the greatest of crimes - and, greatest of all, faithlessness in love.

Let a man be brave, honest, discreet, faithful, and a woman will forgive him all manner of evil actions, even to murder and bloodshed; but let him flinch in danger, lie to save himself, tell the name of a woman whose love for him has betrayed her, or break his faith to her without boldly saying that he loves her no more, and she will not forgive him while he lives, though she may give him a kindly thought and a few tears when he is gone for ever.

So Beatrice, who could never love Ruggiero, understood him well and judged him rightly, and set him up on a sort of pedestal as the anti-type of his scheming master. And not only this. She felt deeply for him and pitied him with all her heart, since she had seen his own almost breaking before her eyes for her sake. She had always been kind to him, but henceforth there would be something even kinder in her voice when she spoke to him, as there would be something harder in her tone when she talked with San Miniato.

And now her mother had appeared and settled herself in her lazy way upon her long chair, and slowly moved her fan, from habit, though too indolent to lift it to her face. Beatrice rose and kissed her lightly on the forehead.

"Good morning, mamma carissima," she said. "Are you very tired after the excursion?"

"Exhausted, in mind and body, my angel. A cigarette, my dear - it will give me an appetite."

Beatrice brought her one, and held a match for her mother.

Then the Marchesa shut her eyes, inhaled the smoke and blew out four or five puffs before speaking again.

"I want to speak to you, my child," she said at last, "but I hardly have the strength."

"Do not tire yourself, mamma. I know what you are going to say, and I have made up my mind."

"Have you? That will save me infinite trouble. I am so glad."

"Are you really? Do you know what I mean?"

"Of course. You are going to marry San Miniato, and we have the best excuse in the world for going to Paris to see about your trousseau."

"I will not marry San Miniato," said Beatrice. "I have made up my mind that I will not."

The Marchesa started slightly as she took her cigarette from her lips, and turned her head slowly so that she could look into Beatrice's eyes.

"You are engaged to marry him," she said slowly. "You cannot break your word. You know what that means. Indeed, you are quite mad!"

"Engaged? I? I never gave my word! It is not true!" The blood rose, in Beatrice's face and then sank suddenly away.

"What is this comedy?" asked the Marchesa, raising her brows. For the first time in many years she was almost angry.

"Ah! If you ask me that, I will tell you. I will tell you everything and you know that I speak the truth to you as I do to everybody -"

"Except to San Miniato when you tell him you love him,"

interrupted the Marchesa.

Beatrice blushed again, with anger this time.

"Yes," she said, after a short pause, "it is quite true that I said I loved him, and for one moment I meant it. But I made a mistake. I am sorry, and I will tell him so. But I will tell him other things, too. I will tell him that I saw through his acting before we left Tragara last night, and that I will never forgive him for the part he played. You know as well as I that it was all a play, from beginning to end. I liked him better than the others because I thought him more manly, more honest, more dignified. But I have changed my mind. I see the whole truth now, every detail of it. He planned it all, and he did it very well - probably he planned it the night before last, out here with you, while I was playing waltzes. You could not make me marry him, and he got leave of you to speak to me. Do you think I do not understand it all? Would you have let me go away last night and sit with him on the rocks, out of your hearing, without so much as a remark, unless you had arranged the matter between you? It is not like you, and I know you meant it. It was all a plot. He had even been there to study the place, to see the very point at which the moon would rise, the very place where he would make me sit, the very spot where your table could stand. He said to himself that I was a mere girl, that of course no man had ever made love to me and that between the beauty of the night, my liking for him, and his well arranged comedy, he might easily move me. He did. I am ashamed of it. Look at the blood in my cheeks! That tells the truth, at all events. I am utterly ashamed. I would give my right hand to have not spoken those words! I would almost give my life to undo yesterday if it could be undone - and undo it I will, so far as I can. I will tell San Miniato what I think of myself, and then I will tell him what I think of him, and that will be enough. Do you understand me? I am in earnest."

The Marchesa had listened to Beatrice's long speech with open eyes, surprised at the girl's keenness and at her determined

　　　　　F. Marion Crawford

manner. Not that the latter was new in her experience, but it was the first time that their two wills had been directly opposed in a matter of great importance. The Marchesa was a very indolent person, but somewhere in her nature there lay hidden a small store of determination which had hardly ever expressed itself clearly in her life. Now, however, she felt that much was at stake. For many reasons San Miniato was precisely the son-in-law she desired. He would give Beatrice an ancient and honourable name, a leading position in any Italian society he chose to frequent, whether in the north or the south, and he was a man of the world at all points. The last consideration had much weight with the Marchesa who, in spite of her title and fortune had seen very little of the men of the great world, and admired them accordingly. Therefore when Beatrice said she would not marry him, her mother made up her mind that she should, and the struggle commenced.

"Beatrice, my angel," she began, "you are mistaken in yourself and in San Miniato. I am quite unable to go through all the details as you have done. I only say that you are mistaken."

Beatrice's lip curled a little and she slowly shook her head.

"I am not mistaken, mamma," she answered. "I am quite right, and you know it. Can you deny that what I say is true? Can you say that you did not arrange with him to take me to Tragara, and to let him speak to me himself?"

"It is far too much trouble to deny anything, my dear child. But all that may be quite true, and yet he may love you as sincerely as he can love any one. I do not suppose you expect a man of his sense and education to roll himself at your feet and tear his hair and his clothes as they do on the stage."

"A man need not do that to show that he is in earnest, and besides he -"

"That is not the question," interrupted the Marchesa. "The real question concerns you much more than it affects him. If you break your promise -"

"There was no promise."

"You told him that you loved him, and you admit it. Under the circumstances that meant that you were willing to marry him. It meant nothing else, as you know very well."

"I never thought of it."

"You must think of it now. You know perfectly well that he wished to marry you and had my consent. I have spoken to you several times about it and you refused to have him, saying that you meant to exercise your own free will. You had an opportunity of exercising it last night. You told him clearly that you loved him, and that could only mean that your opposition was gone and that you would marry him. You know what you will be called now, if you refuse to keep your engagement."

Beatrice grew slowly pale. Her mother had, for once, a remarkably direct and clear way of putting the matter, and the young girl began to waver. If her mother succeeded in proving to her that she had really bound herself, she would submit. It is not easy to convey to the foreign mind generally the enormous importance which is attached in Italy to a distinct promise of marriage. It indeed almost amounts, morally speaking, to marriage itself, and the breaking of it is looked upon socially almost as an act of infidelity to the marriage bond. A young girl who refuses to keep her engagement is called a civetta - an owlet - probably because owlets are used as a decoy all over the country in snaring and shooting all small birds. Be that as it may, the term is a bitter reproach, it sticks to her who has earned it and often ruins her whole life. That is what the Marchesa meant when she told Beatrice that she knew what the world would call her, and the threat had weight.

The young girl rose from her seat and began to walk to and fro

F. Marion Crawford

on the terrace, her head bent, her hands clasped together. The Marchesa slowly puffed at her cigarette and watched her daughter with half-closed eyes.

"I never meant it so!" Beatrice exclaimed in low tones, and she repeated the words again and again, pausing now and then and looking fixedly at her mother.

"Dear child," said the Marchesa, "what does it matter? If it were not such an exertion to talk, I am sure I could make you see what a good match it is, and how glad you ought to be."

"Glad! Oh, mamma, you do not understand! The degradation of it!"

"The degradation? Where is there anything degrading in it?"

"I see it well enough! To give myself up body and soul to a man I do not love! And for what? Because he has an old name, and I a new one, and I can buy his name with my money. Oh, mother, it is too horrible! Too low! Too vile!"

"My angel, you do not know what strong words you are using -"

"They are not half strong enough - I wish I could -"

But she stopped and began to walk up and down again, her sweet young face pale and weary with pain, her fingers twisting each other nervously. A long silence followed.

"It is of no use to talk about it, my child," said the Marchesa, languidly taking up a novel from the table beside her. "The thing is done. You are engaged, and you must either marry San Miniato or take the consequences and be pointed at as a faithless girl for the rest of your life."

"And who knows of this engagement, if it is one, but you and I and he?" asked Beatrice, standing still. "Would you tell, or I?

Or would he dare?"

"He would be perfectly justified," answered the Marchesa. "He is a gentleman, however, and would be considerate. But who is to assure us that he has not already telegraphed the good news to his friends?"

"It is too awful!" cried Beatrice, leaning back against one of the pillars.

"Besides," said her mother without changing her tone. "You have changed to-day, you may change again to-morrow -"

"Stop, for heaven's sake! Do not make me worse than I am!"

Poor Beatrice stopped her ears with her open hands. The Marchesa looked at her and smiled a little, and shook her head, waiting for the hands to be removed. At last the young girl began her walk again.

"You should not talk about being worse when you are not bad at all, my dear," said her mother. "You have done nothing to be ashamed of, and all this is perfectly absurd. You feel a passing dislike for the idea perhaps, but that will be gone to-morrow. Meanwhile the one thing which is really sure is that you are engaged to San Miniato, who, as I say, has undoubtedly telegraphed the fact to his sister in Florence and probably to two or three old friends. By to-morrow it will be in the newspapers. You cannot possibly draw back. I have really talked enough. I am utterly exhausted."

Beatrice sank into a chair and pressed her fingers upon her eyes, not to hide them, but by sheer pressure forcing back the tears she felt coming. Her beautiful young figure bent and trembled like a willow in the wind, and the soft white throat swelled with the choking sob she kept down so bravely. There is something half divine in the grief of some women.

"Dear child," said her mother very gently, "there is nothing to cry over. Beatrice carissima, try and control yourself. It will soon pass -"

"It will soon pass - yes," answered the young girl, bringing out the words with a great effort. During fully two minutes more she pressed her eyes with all her might. Then she rose suddenly to her feet, and her face was almost calm again.

"I will marry him, since what I never meant for a promise really is one and has seemed so to you and to him. But if I am a faithless wife to him, I will lay all my sins at your door."

"Beatrice!" cried the Marchesa, in real horror this time. She crossed herself.

"I am young - shall I not love?" asked the young girl defiantly.

"Dearest child, for the love of Heaven do not talk so -"

"No - I will not. I will never say it again - and you will not forget it."

She turned to leave the terrace and met San Miniato face to face.

"Good morning," she said coldly, and passed him.

"Of course you have telegraphed the news of the engagement to your sister?" said the Marchesa as soon as she saw him, and making a sign to intimate that he must answer in the affirmative.

"Of course - and to all my best friends," he replied promptly with a ready smile. Beatrice heard his answer just as she passed through the door, but she did not turn her head. She guessed that her mother had asked the question in haste in order that San Miniato might say something which should definitely prove to Beatrice that he considered himself betrothed. Yesterday she would have believed his answer. To-day she believed nothing he said. She went to her room and bathed her eyes in cold water and sat down for a moment before her glass and looked at herself thoughtfully. There she was, the same Beatrice she saw in the mirror every day, the same clear brown eyes, the same soft brown hair, the same broad, crayon-like eyebrows, the same free pose of the head. But there was something different in the face, which she did not recognise. There was something defiant in the eyes, and hard about the mouth, which was new to her and did not altogether please her, though she could not change it. She combed the little ringlets on her forehead and dabbed a little scent upon her temples to cool them, and then she rose quickly and went out. A thought had struck her and she at once put into execution the plan it suggested.

She took a parasol and went out of the hotel, hatless and gloveless, into the garden of orange trees which lies between the buildings and the gate. She strolled leisurely along the path towards the exit, on one side of which is the porter's lodge, while the little square stone box of a building which is the telegraph office stands on the other. She knew that just before twelve o'clock Ruggiero and his brother were generally seated on the bench before the lodge waiting for orders for the afternoon. As she expected, she found them, and she beckoned to Ruggiero and turned back under the trees. In an instant he was at her side. She was startled to see how pale he was and how suddenly his face seemed to have grown thin. She stopped and he stood respectfully before her, cap in hand, looking down.

"Ruggiero," she said, "will you do me a service?"

"Yes, Excellency."

"Yes, I know - but it is something especial. You must tell no one - not even your brother."

"Speak, Excellency - not even the stones shall hear it."

"I want you to find out at the telegraph office whether your master has sent a telegram anywhere this morning. Can you ask the man and bring me word here? I will walk about under the trees."

"At once, Excellency."

He turned and left her, and she strolled up the path. She wondered a little why she was doing this underhand thing. It was not like her, and whatever answer Ruggiero brought her she would gain nothing by it. If San Miniato had spoken the truth, then he had really believed the engagement already binding, as her mother had said. If he had lied, that would not prevent his really telegraphing within the next half hour, and matters would be in just the same situation with a slight difference of time. She would, indeed, in this latter case, have a fresh proof of his duplicity. But she needed none, as it seemed to her. It was enough that he should have acted his comedy last night and got by a stratagem what he could never have by any other means. Ruggiero returned after two or three minutes.

"Well?" inquired Beatrice.

"He sent one at nine o'clock this morning, Excellency."

For one minute their eyes met. Ruggiero's were fierce, bright and clear. Beatrice's own softened almost imperceptibly under his glance. If she had seen herself at that moment she would have noticed that the hard look she had observed in her own face had momentarily vanished, and that she was her gentle self again.

"One only?" she asked.

"Only one, Excellency. No one will know that I have asked, for the man will not tell."

"Are you sure? What did you say to him? Tell me."

"I said to him, 'Don Gennaro, I am the Conte di San Miniato's sailor. Has the Conte sent any telegram this morning, to any one, anywhere?' Then he shook his head; but he looked into his book and said, 'He sent one to Florence at nine o'clock.' Then I said, 'I thank you, Don Gennaro, and I will do you a service when I can.' That was for good manners. Then I said, 'Don Gennaro, please not to tell any one that I asked the question, and if you tell any one I will make you die an evil death, for I will break all your bones and moreover drown you in the sea, and go to the galleys very gladly.' Then Don Gennaro said that he would not tell. And here I am, Excellency."

In spite of all she was suffering, Beatrice laughed at Ruggiero's account of the interview. It was quite evident that Ruggiero had repeated accurately every word that had been spoken, and he looked the man to execute the threat without the slightest hesitation. Beatrice wondered how the telegraph official had taken it.

"What did Don Gennaro do when you frightened him, Ruggiero?" she asked.

"He said he would not tell and got a little white, Excellency. But he will say nothing, and will not complain to the syndic, because he knows my brother."

"What has that to do with it?" asked Beatrice with some curiosity.

"It is natural, Excellency. For if Don Gennaro went to the syndic and said, 'Signor Sindaco, Ruggiero of the Children of the King has threatened to kill me,' then the syndic would send for the gendarmes and say, 'Take that Ruggiero of the Children of the King and put him in, as we say, and see that he does not run away, for he will do a hurt to somebody.' And perhaps they would catch me and perhaps they would not. Then Bastianello, my brother, would wait in the road in the evening for Don Gennaro, and would lay a hand on him, perhaps, or both. And I think that Don Gennaro would rather be dead in his telegraph office than alive in Bastianello's hands, because Bastianello is very strong in his hands, Excellency. And that is all the truth."

"But I do not understand it all, Ruggiero, though I see what you mean. I am afraid it is your language that is different from mine."

"It is natural, Excellency," answered the sailor, a deep blush spreading over his white forehead as he stood bareheaded before her. "You are a great lady and I am only an ignorant seaman."

"I do not mean anything of the sort, Ruggiero," said Beatrice quickly, for she saw that she had unintentionally hurt him, and the thought pained her strongly. "You speak very well and I have always understood you perfectly. But you spoke of the King's Children and I could not make out what they had to do with the story."

"Oh, if it is that, Excellency, I ask your pardon. I do not wonder that you did not understand. It is my name, Excellency."

"Your name? Still I do not understand -"

"I have no other name but that - dei figli del Re -" said Ruggiero. "That is all."

"How strange!" exclaimed Beatrice.

"It is the truth, Excellency, and to show you that it is the truth here is my seaman's license."

He produced a little flat parchment case from his pocket, untied the thong and showed Beatrice the first page on which, was inscribed his name in full.

"Ruggiero of the Children of the King, son of the late Ruggiero, native of Verbicaro, province of Calabria - you see, Excellency. It is the truth."

"I never doubt anything you say, Ruggiero," said Beatrice quietly.

"I thank you, Excellency," answered the sailor, blushing this time with pleasure. "For this and all your Excellency's kindness."

What a man he was she thought, as he stood there before her, bareheaded in the sun-shot shade under the trees, the light playing upon his fair hair and beard, and his blue eyes gleaming like drops from the sea! What boys and dwarfs other men looked beside him!

"Do you know how your family came by that strange name, Ruggiero?" she asked.

"No, Excellency. But they tell so many silly stories about us in Verbicaro. That is in Calabria where I and my brother were born. And when our mother, blessed soul, was dying - good health to your Excellency - she blessed us and said this to us. 'Ruggiero, Sebastiano, dear sons, you could not save me and I am going. God bless you,' said she. 'Our Lady help you. Remember, you are the Children of the King.' Then she said, 'Remember' again, as though she would say something more. But just at that very moment Christ took her, and she did not speak again, for she was dead - good health to your Excellency for a thousand years. And so it was."

"And what happened then?" asked Beatrice, strangely interested and charmed by the man's simple story.

"Then we beat Don Pietro Casale, Excellency, and spoiled all his face and head. We were little boys, twelve and ten years old, but there was the anger to give us strength. And so we ran away from Verbicaro, because we had no one and we had to

F. Marion Crawford

eat, and had beaten Don Pietro Casale, who would have had us put in prison if he had caught us. But thanks to Heaven we had good legs. And so we ran away, Excellency."

"It is very interesting. But what were those stories they told about you in Verbicaro?"

"Silly stories, Excellency. They say that once upon a time King Roger came riding by with all his army and many knights; and all armed because there was war. And he took Verbicaro from the Turks and gave it to a son of his who was called the Son of the King, as I would give Bastianello half a cigar or a pipe of tobacco in the morning - it is true he always has his own - and so the Son of the King stayed in that place and lived there, and I have heard old men say that when their fathers - who were also old, Excellency - were boys, many houses in Verbicaro belonged to the Children of the King. But then they ate everything and we have had nothing but these two hands and these two arms and now we go about seeking to eat. But thanks to Heaven - and to-day is Saturday - we have been able to work enough. And that is the truth, Excellency."

"What a strange tale!" exclaimed the young girl. "But to-day is Tuesday, Ruggiero. Why do you say it is Saturday?"

"I beg pardon of your Excellency, it is a silly custom and means nothing. But when a man says he is well, or that there is a west wind, or that his boat is sound, he says 'to-day is Saturday,' because it might be Friday and he might have forgotten that. It is a silly custom, Excellency."

"Do not call me excellency, Ruggiero," said Beatrice. "I have no right to be called so."

"And what could I call you when I have to speak to you, Excellency? I have been taught so."

"Only princes and dukes and their children are excellencies," answered Beatrice. "My father was only a Marchese. So if you wish to please me, call me 'signorina.' That is the proper way to speak to me."

"I will try, Excellency," answered Ruggiero, opening his blue eyes very wide. Beatrice laughed a little.

"You see," she said, "you did it again."

"Yes, Signorina," replied Ruggiero. "But I will not forget again. When the tongue of the ignorant has learned a word it is hard to change it."

"Well, good-day Ruggiero. Your story is very interesting. I am going to breakfast, and I thank you for what you did for me."

"It is not I who deserve any thanks. And good appetite to you, Signorina." She turned and walked slowly back towards the hotel.

"And may Our Lady bless you and keep you, and send an angel to watch over every hair of your blessed head!" said Ruggiero in a low voice as he watched her graceful figure retreating in the distance.

F. Marion Crawford

CHAPTER IX

After what had happened on the previous evening Ruggiero had expected that Beatrice would treat him very differently. He had assuredly not foreseen that she would call him from his seat by the porter's lodge, ask an important service of him, and then enter into conversation with him about the origin of his family and the story of his own life. His slow but logical mind pondered on these things in spite of the disordered action of his heart, which had almost choked him while he had been talking with the young girl. Instead of going back to his brother, he turned aside and entered the steep descending tunnel through the rock which leads down to the sea and the little harbour.

Two things were strongly impressed on his mind. First, the nature of the service he had done Beatrice in making that enquiry at the telegraph office, and secondly her readiness to forget his own reckless conduct at Tragara. Both these points suggested reflections which pleased him strangely. It was quite clear to him that Beatrice distrusted San Miniato, though he had of course no idea of the nature of the telegram concerning which she had wanted information. He only understood that she was watching San Miniato with suspicion, expecting some sort of foul play. But there was an immense satisfaction in that thought, and Ruggiero's eyes sparkled as he revolved it in his brain.

As for the other matter, he understood it less clearly. He was quite conscious of the enormity of his misdeed in telling a lady, and a great lady, according to his view, that he loved her, and in daring to touch the sleeves of her dress with his rough hands. He could not find it in him to regret what he had done, but he was prepared for very hard treatment as his just reward. It would not have surprised him if Beatrice had then and there complained of him to her mother or to San Miniato himself, and the latter, Ruggiero supposed, would have had no difficulty in having him locked up in the town gaol for a few weeks on the rather serious ground of misdemeanour towards the visitors at the watering-place. A certain amount of rather arbitrary power is placed in the hands of the local authorities in all great summer resorts, and it is quite right that it should be so - nor is it as a rule unjustly used.

But Beatrice had acted very differently, very kindly and very generously. That was because she was naturally so good and gentle, thought Ruggiero. But the least he had expected was that she would never again speak to him save to give an order, nor say a kind word, no matter what service he rendered her, or what danger he ran for her sake. And now, a moment ago, she had talked with him with more interest and kindly condescension than she had ever shown before. He refused, and rightly, to believe that this was because she had needed his help in the matter of the telegram. She could have called Bastianello, who was in her own service, and Bastianello would have done just as well. But she had chosen to employ the man who had so rudely forgotten himself before her less than twenty-four hours earlier. Why? Ruggiero, little capable, by natural gifts or by experience, of dealing with such questions, found himself face to face with a great problem of the human self, and he knew at once that he could never solve it, try as he might. His happiness was none the less great, nor his gratitude the less deep and sincere, and with both these grew up instantly in his heart the strong determination to serve her at every turn, so far as lay in his power.

It was not much that he could do, he reflected, unless she would show him the way as she had done this very morning. But, considering the position of affairs, and her evident distrust of her betrothed, it was not impossible that similar situations might arise before long. If they did, Ruggiero would be ready, as he had now shown himself, to do her bidding with startling directness and energy. He was well aware of his physical superiority over every one else in Sorrento, and he was dimly conscious that a threat from him was something which would frighten most men, and which none could afford to overlook. He remembered poor Don Gennaro's face just now, when he had quietly told him what he might expect if he did not hold his tongue. Ruggiero had never valued his life very highly, and since he had loved Beatrice he did not value it a straw. This state of mind can make a man an exceedingly dangerous person, especially when he is so endowed that he can tear a new horse shoe in two with his hands, and break a five franc piece with his thumbs and forefingers as another man breaks a biscuit.

As Ruggiero came out of the tunnel and reached the platform of rock from which the last part of the descent goes down to the sea in the open air, he stood still a moment and expressed his determination in a low tone. There was no one near to hear him.

"Whatever she asks," he said. "Truly it is of great importance what becomes of me! If it is a little thing it costs nothing. If it is a great thing - well, I will do it if I can. Then I will say, 'Excellency' - no - 'Signorina, here it is done. And I beg to kiss your Excellency's hand, because I am going to the galleys and you will not see me any more.' And then they will put me in, and it will be finished, and I shall always have the satisfaction."

Ruggiero produced a fragment of a cigar from his cap and a match from the same safe place and began to smoke, looking at the sea. People not used to the peculiarities of southern thought would perhaps have been surprised at the desperate simplicity of Ruggiero's statement to himself. But those who have been long familiar with men of his country and class must all have heard exactly such words uttered more than once in their experience, and will remember that in some cases at least they were not empty threats, which were afterwards very exactly and conscientiously fulfilled by him who uttered them, and who now either wears a green cap at Ponza or Ischia, or is making a fortune in South America, having had the luck to escape as a stowaway on a foreign vessel.

Nor did it strike Ruggiero as at all improbable that Beatrice might some day wish to be rid of the Conte di San Miniato, and might express such a wish, ever so vaguely, within Ruggiero's hearing. He had the bad taste to judge her by himself, and of course if she really hated her betrothed she would wish him to die. It was a sin, doubtless, to wish anybody dead, and it was a greater sin to put out one's hands and kill the person in question. But it was human nature, according to Ruggiero's simple view, and of course Beatrice felt like other human beings in this matter and all the principal affairs of life. He had made up his mind, and he never repeated the words he had spoken to himself. He was a simple man, and he puffed at his stump of a black cigar and strolled down to the boat to find out whether the Cripple and the Son of the Fool had spliced that old spare mooring-rope which had done duty last night and had been found chafed this morning.

Meanwhile the human nature on which Ruggiero counted so naturally and confidently was going through a rather strange phase of development in the upper regions where the Marchesa's terrace was situated.

Beatrice walked slowly back under the trees. Ruggiero's quaint talk had amused her and had momentarily diverted the current of her thoughts. But the moment she left him, her mind reverted to her immediate trouble, and she felt a little stab of pain at the heart which was new to her. The news that San Miniato had actually sent a telegram was unwelcome in the extreme. He had, indeed, said in her presence that he had sent several. But that might have been a careless inaccuracy, or he might have actually written the rest and given them to be despatched before coming upstairs. To doubt that the one message already sent contained the news of his engagement,

F. Marion Crawford

seemed gratuitous. It was only too sure that he had looked upon what had passed at Tragara as a final decision on the part of Beatrice, and that henceforth she was his affianced bride. Her mother had not even found great difficulty in persuading her of the fact, and after that one bitter struggle she had given up the battle. It had been bitter indeed while it had lasted, and some of the bitterness returned upon her now. But she would not again need to force the tears back, pressing her hands upon her eyes with desperate strength as she had done. It was useless to cry over what could not be helped, and since she had made the great mistake of her life she must keep her word or lose her good name for ever, according to the ideas in which she had been brought up. But it would be very hard to meet San Miniato now, within the next quarter of an hour, as she inevitably must. Less hard, perhaps, than if she had convicted him of falsehood in the matter of the telegram, as she had fully expected that she could - but painful enough, heaven knew.

There was an old trace of oriental fatalism in her nature, passed down to her, perhaps, from some Saracen ancestor in the unknown genealogy of her family. It is common enough in the south, often profoundly leavened with superstition, sometimes existing side by side with the most absolute scepticism, but its influence is undeniable, and accounts for a certain resignation in hopeless cases which would be utterly foreign to the northern character. Beatrice had it, and having got the worst of the first contest she conceived that further resistance would be wholly useless, and accepted the inevitable conclusion that she must marry San Miniato whether she liked him or not. But this state of mind did not by any means imply that she would marry him with a good grace, or ever again return in her behaviour towards him to the point she had reached on the previous evening. That, thought Beatrice, would be too much to expect, and was certainly more than she intended to give. She would be quite willing to show that she had been deceived into consenting, and was only keeping her word as a matter of principle. San Miniato might think what he pleased. She knew that whatever she did, he would never think of breaking off the engagement, since what he wanted was not herself but her fortune. She shut her parasol with a rather vicious snap as she went into the cool hall out of the sun, and the hard look in her face was more accentuated than before, as she slowly ascended the steps.

The conversation between her mother and San Miniato during her short absence had been characteristic. They understood each other perfectly but neither would have betrayed to the other, by the merest hint, the certainty that the marriage was by no means agreeable to poor Beatrice herself.

"Dearest Marchesa," said San Miniato, touching her hand with his lips, and then seating himself beside her, "tell me that you are not too much exhausted after your exertions last night? Have you slept well? Have you any appetite?"

"What a good doctor you would make, dear friend!" exclaimed the Marchesa with a little smile.

And so they exchanged the amenities usual at their first meeting in the day, as though they had not been buying and selling an innocent soul, and did not appreciate the fact in its startling reality. Several more phrases of the same kind were spoken.

"And how is Donna Beatrice?" inquired San Miniato at last.

"Why not call her Beatrice?" asked the Marchesa carelessly. "She is very well. You just saw her."

"I fancy it would seem a little premature, a little familiar to call her so," answered the Count, who remembered his recent discomfiture. "For the present, I believe she would prefer a little more ceremony. I do not know whether I am right. Pray give me your advice, Marchesa carissima."

"Of course you are right - you always are. You were right about the moon yesterday - though I did not notice that it was shining here when we came home," she added thoughtfully, not by any means satisfied with the insufficient demonstration he had given her at first.

"No doubt," replied San Miniato indifferently. He took no further interest in the movements of the satellite since he had gained his point, and the Marchesa was far too lazy to revive the discussion. "I am glad you agree with me about my behaviour," he continued. "It is of course most important to maintain as much as possible the good impression I was so fortunate as to make last night, and I have had enough experience of the world to know that it will not be an easy matter."

"No, indeed - and with Beatrice's character, too!"

"The most charming character I ever met," said San Miniato with sufficient warmth. "But young, of course, as it should be and subject to the enchanting little caprices which belong to youth and beauty."

"Yes, which always belong to youth and beauty," assented the Marchesa.

"And I am quite prepared, for instance, to be treated coldly to-day and warmly to-morrow, if it so pleases the dear young lady. She will always find me the same."

"How good you are, dearest friend!" exclaimed the Marchesa, thoroughly understanding what he meant, and grateful to him for his tact, which was sometimes, indeed, of the highest order.

"It would be strange if I were not happy and satisfied," he answered, "and ready to accept gratefully the smallest favour with which it may please Donna Beatrice to honor me."

He was indeed both happy and satisfied, for he saw no reason to suppose that the Granmichele fortune could now slip from his grasp. Moreover he had considerable confidence in himself and his powers, and he thought it quite probable that the scene of the previous evening might before long be renewed with more lasting effect. Beatrice was young and capricious; there is nothing one may count on so surely as youth and caprice. Caprice is sure to change, but who is sure that the faith kept for ten years will not? In youth love is sure to come some day, but when that day is past is it ever sure that he will come again? San Miniato knew these things and many more like them, and was wise in his generation as well as a man of the world, accustomed to its ways from his childhood and nourished with the sour milk of its wisdom from his earliest youth upward.

So he quietly conveyed to the Marchesa the information that he understood Beatrice's present mood and that he would not attach more importance to it than it deserved. They talked a little longer together, both for the present avoiding any reference to the important arrangements which must soon be discussed in connection with the marriage contract, but both taking it entirely for granted that the marriage itself was quite agreed upon and settled.

Then Beatrice returned and sat down silently by the table.

"Have you been for a little walk, my angel?" enquired her mother.

"Yes, mamma, I have been for a little walk."

"You are not tired then, after our excursion, Donna Beatrice?" enquired San Miniato.

"Not in the least," answered the young girl, taking up a book and beginning to read.

"Beatrice!" exclaimed her mother in amazement. "My child! What are you reading! Maupassant! Have you quite forgotten yourself?"

"I am trying to, mamma. And since I am to be married - what

difference does it make?"

She spoke without laying down the volume. San Miniato pretended to pay no attention to the incident, and slowly rolled a fat cigarette between his fingers to soften it before smoking. The Marchesa made gestures to Beatrice with an unusual expenditure of energy, but with no effect.

"It seems very interesting," said the latter. "I had no idea he wrote so well. It seems to be quite different from Telemaque - more amusing in every way."

Then the Marchesa did what she had not done in many years. She asserted her parental authority. Very lazily she put her feet to the ground, laid her fan, her handkerchief and her cigarette case together, and rose to her feet. Coming round the table she took the forbidden book out of Beatrice's hands, shut it up and put it back in its place. Beatrice made no opposition, but raised her broad eyebrows wearily and folded her hands in her lap.

"Of course, if you insist, I have nothing to say," she remarked, "any more than I have anything to do since you will not let me read."

The Marchesa went back to her lounge and carefully arranged her belongings and settled herself comfortably before she spoke.

"I think you are a little out of temper, Beatrice dear, or perhaps you are hungry, my child. You so often are. San Miniato, what time is it?"

"A quarter before twelve," answered the Count.

"Of course you will breakfast with us. Ring the bell, dearest friend. We will not wait any longer."

San Miniato rose and touched the button.

"You are as hospitable as you are good," he said. "But if you will forgive me, I will not accept your invitation to-day. An old friend of mine is at the other hotel for a few hours and I have promised to breakfast with him. Will you excuse me?"

Beatrice made an almost imperceptible gesture of indifference with her hand.

"Who is your friend?" she asked.

"A Piedmontese," answered San Miniato indifferently. "You do not know him."

"We are very sorry to lose you, especially to-day, San Miniato carissimo," said the Marchesa. "But if it cannot be helped - well, good-bye."

So San Miniato went out and left the mother and daughter together again as he had found them. It is needless to say that the Piedmontese friend was a fiction, and that San Miniato had no engagement of that kind. He had hastily resolved to keep one of a different nature because he guessed that in Beatrice's present temper he would make matters more difficult by staying. And in this he was right, for Beatrice had made up her mind to be thoroughly disagreeable and she possessed the elements of success requisite for that purpose - a sharp tongue, a quick instinct and great presence of mind.

San Miniato descended the stairs and strolled out into the orange garden, looking at his watch as he left the door of the hotel. It was very hot, but further away from the house the sea breeze was blowing through the trees. He was still smoking the cigarette he had lighted upstairs, and he sat down on a bench in the shade, took out a pocket book and began to make notes. From time to time he looked along the path in the direction of the hotel, which was hidden from view by the shrubbery. Then the clock struck twelve and a few minutes later the church bells began to ring, as they do half a dozen times a day in Italy on small provocation. Still San Miniato went on with his calculations.

Before many minutes more had passed, a trim young figure appeared in the path - a young girl, with pink cheeks and bright dark eyes, no other than Teresina, the Marchesa's maid. She carried some sewing in her hand and looked nervously behind her and to the right and left as she walked. But there was no one in the garden at that hour. The guests of the hotel were all at breakfast, and the servants were either asleep or at work indoors. The porter was at his dinner and the sailors were presumably eating their midday bread and cheese down by the boats, or dining at their homes if they lived near by. The breeze blew pleasantly through the trees, making the broad polished leaves rustle and the little green oranges rock on the boughs.

As soon as San Miniato caught sight of Teresina he put his note-book into his pocket and rose to his feet. His face betrayed neither pleasure nor surprise as he sauntered along the path, until he was close to her. Then both stopped, and he smiled, bending down and looking into her eyes.

"For charity's sake, Signor Conte!" cried the girl, drawing back, blushing and looking behind her quickly. "I ought never to have come here. Why did you make me come?"

"What an idea, Teresina!" laughed San Miniato softly. "And if you ask me why I wanted you to come, here is the reason. Now tell me, Teresinella, is it a good reason or not?"

Thereupon San Miniato produced from his waistcoat pocket a little limp parcel wrapped in white tissue paper and laid it in Teresina's hand. It was heavy, and she guessed that it contained something of gold.

"What is it?" she asked quickly. "Am I to give it to the Signorina?"

"To the Signorina!" San Miniato laughed softly again and laid his hand very gently on the girl's arm. "Yes," he whispered, bending down to her. "To the Signorina Teresinella, who can have all she asks for if she will only care a little for me."

"Heavens, Signor Conte!" cried Teresina. "Was it to say this that you made me come?"

"This and a great deal more, Teresina bella. Open your little parcel while I tell you the rest. Who made you so pretty, carissima? Nature knew what she was doing when she made those eyes of yours and those bright cheeks, and those little hands and this small waist - per Dio - if some one I know were as pretty as Teresinella, all Naples would be at her feet!"

He slipped his arm round her, there in the shade. Still she held the package unopened in her hand. She grew a little pale, as he touched her, and shrank away as though to avoid him, but evidently uncertain and deeply disturbed. The poor girl's good and evil angels were busy deciding her fate for her at that moment.

"Open your little gift and see whether you like the reason I give you for coming here," said San Miniato, who was pleased with the turn of the phrase and thought it as well to repeat it. "Open it, Teresinella, bella, bella - the first of as many as you like - and come and sit beside me on the bench there and let me talk a little. I have so much to say to you, all pretty things which you will like, and the hour is short, you know."

Poor girl! He was a fine gentleman with a very great name, as Teresina knew, and he was young still and handsome, and had winning ways, and she loved gold and pretty speeches dearly. She looked down, still shrinking away from him, till she stood with her back to a tree. Her fresh young face was almost white now and her eyelids trembled from time to time, while her lips moved though she was not conscious of what she wanted to say.

"Ah, Teresina!" he exclaimed, with a nicely adjusted cadence of passion in the tone. "What are you waiting for, my little angel? It is time to love when one is young and the world is green, and your eyes are bright, carina! When the heart beats and the blood is warm! And you are made for love - that mouth of yours - like the red carnations - one kiss Teresinella - that is all I ask - one kiss and no more, - here in the shade while no one is looking - one kiss, carina mia - there is no sin in kissing -"

And he tried to draw her to him. But either Teresina was naturally a very good girl, or her good angel had demolished his evil adversary in the encounter which had taken place. There is an odd sort of fierce loyalty very often to be found at the root of the Sicilian character. She looked up suddenly and her eyes met his. She held out the little package still unopened.

"You have made a mistake, Signor Conte," she said, quietly enough. "I am an honest girl, and though you are a great signore I will tell you that if you had any honour you would not be making love to me out here in the garden while you are paying court to the Signorina when you are in the house, and doing your best to marry her. It is infamous enough, what you are doing, and I am not afraid to tell you so. And take back your gold, for I do not want it, and it is not clean! And so good-day, Signor Conte, and many thanks. When you asked me to come here, I thought you had some private message for the Signorina."

During Teresina's speech San Miniato had not betrayed the slightest surprise or disappointment. He quietly lighted a cigarette and smiled good-humouredly all the time.

"My dear Teresina," he said, when she had finished, "what in the world do you think I wanted of you? Not only am I paying court to your signorina, as you say, but I am already betrothed to her, since last night. You did not know that?"

"The greater the shame!" exclaimed the girl, growing angry.

"Not at all, my dear child. On the contrary, it explains

everything in the most natural way. Is it not really natural that on the occasion of my betrothal I should wish to give you a little remembrance, because you have always been so obliging, and have been with the Marchesa since you were a child? I could not do anything else, I am sure, and I beg you to keep it and wear it. And as for my telling you that you are pretty and young and fresh, I do not see why you need be so mortally offended at that. However, Teresina, I am sorry if you misunderstood me. You will keep the little chain?"

"No, Signor Conte. Take it. And I do not believe a word you say."

She held out the parcel to him, but he, still smiling, shook his head and would not take it. Then she let it drop at his feet, and turned quickly and left him. He watched her a moment, and his annoyance at his discomfiture showed itself plainly enough, so soon as she was not there to see it. Then he shrugged his shoulders, stooped and picked up the package, restored it to his waistcoat pocket and went back to his bench.

"It is a pity," he muttered, as he took out his note-book again. "It would have been such good practice!"

An hour later Bastianello was sitting alone in the boat, under the awning, enjoying the cool breeze and wishing that the ladies would go for a sail while it lasted, instead of waiting until late in the afternoon as they generally did, at which time there was usually not a breath of air on the water. He was smoking a clay pipe with a cane stem, and he was thinking vaguely of Teresina, wondering whether Ruggiero would never speak to her, and if he never did, whether he, Bastianello, might not at last have his turn.

A number of small boys were bathing in the bright sunshine, diving off the stones of the breakwater and running along the short pier, brown urchins with lithe thin limbs, matted black hair and beady eyes. Suddenly Bastianello was aware of a small dark face and two little hands holding upon the gunwale of his boat. He knew the boy very well, for he was the son of the Son of the Fool.

"Let go, Nenne!" he said; "do you take us for a bathing house?"

"You have a beautiful pair of padroni, you and your brother," observed Nenne, making a hideous face over the boat's side.

Bastianello did not move, but stretched out his long arm to take up the boat-hook, which lay within his reach.

"If you had seen what I saw in the garden up there just now," continued the small boy. "Madonna mia, what a business!"

"Eh, you rascal? what did you see?" asked the sailor, turning the boat-hook round and holding it so that he could rap the boy's knuckles with the butt end of it.

"There was the Count, who is Ruggiero's padrone, trying to kiss your signora's maid, and offering her the gold, and she - yah!" Another hideous grimace, apparently of delight, interrupted the narrative.

"What did she do?" asked Bastianello quietly. But he grew a shade paler.

"Eh? you want to know now, do you? What will you give me?" inquired the urchin.

"Half a cigar," said Bastianello, who knew the boy's vicious tastes, and forthwith produced the bribe from his cap, holding it up for the other to see.

"What did she do? She threw down the gold and called him an infamous liar to his face. A nice padrone Ruggiero has, who is called a liar and an infamous one by serving maids. Well, give me the cigar."

"Take it," said the sailor, rising and reaching out.

The urchin stuck it between his teeth, nodded his thanks, lowered himself gently into the water so as not to wet it, and swam cautiously to the breakwater, holding his head in the air.

Bastianello sat down again and continued to smoke his pipe. There was a happy look in his bright blue eyes which had not been there before.

CHAPTER X

Bastianello sat still in his boat, but he no longer looked to seaward, facing the breeze. He kept an eye on the pier, looking out for his brother, who had not appeared since the midday meal. The piece of information he had just received was worth communicating, for it raised Teresina very much in the eyes of Bastianello, and he did not doubt that it would influence Ruggiero in the right direction. Bastianello, too, was keen enough to see that anything which gave him an opportunity of discussing the girl with his brother might be of advantage, in that it might bring Ruggiero to the open expression of a settled purpose - either to marry the girl or not. And if he once gave his word that he would not, Bastianello would be no longer bound to suffer in silence as he had suffered so many weeks. The younger of the brothers was less passionate, less nervous and less easily moved in every way than the elder, but he possessed much of the same general character and all of the same fundamental good qualities - strength, courage and fidelity. In his quiet way he was deeply and sincerely in love with Teresina, and meant, if possible and if Ruggiero did not take her, to make her his wife.

At last Ruggiero's tall figure appeared at the corner of the building occupied by the coastguard station, and Bastianello immediately whistled to him, giving a signal which had served the brothers since they were children. Ruggiero started, turned his head and at once jumped into the first boat he could lay hands on and pulled out alongside of his brother.

"What is it?" he asked, letting his oars swing astern and laying hold on the gunwale of the sail boat.

"About Teresina," answered Bastianello, taking his pipe from his mouth and leaning towards his brother. "The son of the Son of the Fool was swimming about here just now, and he hauled himself half aboard of me and made faces. So I took the boat-hook to hit his fingers. And just then he said to me, 'You have a beautiful pair of masters you and your brother.' 'Why?' I asked, and I held the boat-hook ready. But I would not have hurt the boy, because he is one of ours. So he told me that he had just seen the Count up there in the garden of the hotel, trying to kiss Teresina and offering her the gold, and I gave him half a cigar to tell me the rest, because he would not, and made faces."

"May he die murdered!" exclaimed Ruggiero in a low voice, his face as white as canvas.

"Wait a little, she is a good girl," answered Bastianello. "Teresina threw the gold upon the ground and told the Count that he was an infamous one and a liar. And then she went away. And I think the boy was speaking the truth, because if it were a lie he would have spoken in another way. For it was as easy to say that the Count kissed her as to say that she would not let him, and he would have had the tobacco all the same."

"May he die of a stroke!" muttered Ruggiero.

"But if I were in your place," said his brother calmly, "I would not do anything to your padrone, because the girl is a good girl and gave him the good answer, and as for him -" Bastianello shrugged his shoulders.

"May the sharks get his body and the devil get his soul!"

"That will be as it shall be," answered Bastianello. "And it is sure that if God wills, the grampuses will eat him. But we do not know the end. What I would say is this, that it is time you should speak to the girl, because I see how white you get when we talk of her, and you are consuming yourself and will have an illness, and though I could work for both you and me, four arms are better than two, in summer as in winter. Therefore I say, go and speak to her, for she will have you and she will be better with you than near that apoplexy of a San Miniato."

Ruggiero did not answer at once, but pulled out his pipe and filled it and began to smoke.

"Why should I speak?" he asked at last. There was a struggle in his mind, for he did not wish to tell Bastianello outright that he did not really care for Teresina. If he betrayed this fact it would be hard hereafter to account for his own state, which was too apparent to be concealed, especially from his brother, and he had no idea that the latter loved the girl.

"Why should you speak?" asked Bastianello, repeating the words, and stirring the ashes in his pipe with the point of his knife. "Because if you do not speak you will never get anything."

"It will be the same if I do," observed Ruggiero stolidly.

"I believe that very little," returned the other. "And I will tell you something. If I were to speak to Teresina for you and say, 'Here is my brother Ruggiero, who is not a great signore, but is well grown and has two arms which are good, and a matter of seven or eight hundred francs in the bank, and who is very fond of you, but he does not know how to say it. Think well if you will have him,' I would say, 'and if you will not, give me an honest answer and God bless you and let it be the end.' That is how I would speak, and she would think about it for a week or perhaps two, and then she would say to me, 'Bastianello, tell your brother that I will have him.' Or else she would say, 'Bastianello, tell your brother that I thank him, but that I have no heart in it.' That is what she would say."

"It may be," said Ruggiero carelessly. "But of course she would thank, and say 'Who is this Ruggiero?' and besides, the world is full of women."

Bastianello was about to ask the interpretation of this rather enigmatical speech when there was a stir on the pier and two or three boats put out, the men standing in them and sculling them stern foremost.

"Who is it?" asked Bastianello of the boatman who passed nearest to him.

"The Giovannina," answered the man.

She had returned from her last voyage to Calabria, having taken macaroni from Amalfi and bringing back wine of Verbicaro. A fine boat, the Giovannina, able to carry twenty tons in any weather, and water-tight too, being decked with hatches over which you can stretch and batten down tarpaulin. A pretty sight as she ran up to the end of the breakwater, old Luigione standing at the stern with the tiller between his knees and the slack of the main-sheet in his hand. She was running wing and wing, with her bright new sails spreading far over the water on each side. Then came a rattle and a sharp creak as the main-yard swung over and came down on deck, the men taking in the bellying canvas with wide open arms and old Luigione catching the end of the yard on his shoulder while he steered with his knees, his great gaunt profile black against the bright sky. Down foresail, and the good felucca forges ahead and rounds the little breakwater. Let go the anchor and she is at rest after her long voyage. For the season has not been good and she has been hauled on a dozen beaches before she could sell her cargo. The men are all as brown as mahogany, and as lean as wolves, for it has been a voyage with share and share alike for all the crew and they have starved themselves to bring home more money to their wives.

Then there is some bustle and confusion, as Luigione brings the papers ashore and friends crowd around the felucca in boats, asking for news and all talking at once.

"We have been in your town, Ruggiero," said one of the men, looking down into the little boat.

"I hope you gave a message from me to Don Pietro Casale," answered Ruggiero.

"Health to us, Don Pietro is dead," said the man, "and his wife is not likely to live long either."

"Dead, eh?" cried Bastianello. "He is gone to show the saints the nose we gave him when we were boys."

"We can go back to Verbicaro when we please," observed Ruggiero with a smile.

"Lend a hand on board, will you?" said the sailor.

So Ruggiero made the boat fast with the painter and both brothers scrambled over the side of the felucca. They did not renew their conversation concerning Teresina, and an hour or two later they went up to the hotel to be in readiness for their masters, should the latter wish to go out. Ruggiero sat down on a bench in the garden, but Bastianello went into the house.

In the corridor outside the Marchesa's rooms he met Teresina, who stopped and spoke to him as she always did when she met him, for though she admired both the brothers, she liked Bastianello better than she knew - perhaps because he talked more and seemed to have a gentler temper.

"Good-day, Bastianello," she said, with a bright smile.

"And good-day to you, Teresina," answered Bastianello. "Can you tell me whether the padroni will go out to-day in the boat?"

"I think they will not," answered the girl. "But I will ask. But I think they will not, because there is the devil in the house to-day, and the Signorina looks as though she would eat us all, and that is a bad sign."

"What has happened?" asked Bastianello. "You can tell me, because I will tell nobody."

"The truth is this," answered Teresina, lowering her voice. "They have betrothed her to the Count, and she does not like it. But if you say anything - ." She laughed a little and shook her finger at him.

Bastianello threw his head back to signify that he would not repeat what he had heard. Then he gazed into Teresina's eyes for a moment.

"The Count is worse than an animal," he said quietly.

"If you knew how true that is!" exclaimed Teresina, blushing deeply and turning away. "I will ask the Marchesa if she will go out," she added, as she walked quickly away.

Bastianello waited and in a few moments she came back.

"Not to-day," she said.

"So much the better. I want to say something to you, Teresina. Will you listen to me? Can I say it here?" Bastianello felt unaccountably nervous, and when he had spoken he regretted it.

"I hope it is good news," answered the girl. "Come to the window at the end of the corridor. We shall be further from the door there, and there is more air. Now what is it?" she asked as they reached the place she had chosen.

"It is this, Teresina," said Bastianello, summoning all his courage for what was the most difficult undertaking of his life. "You know my brother Ruggiero."

"Eh! I should think so! I see him every day."

"Good. He also sees you every day, and he sees how beautiful you are, and now he knows how good you are, because the little boy of the Son of the Fool saw you with that apoplexy of a Count in the garden to-day, and heard what you said, and came and told me, and I told Ruggiero because I knew how glad he would be."

"Dio mio!" cried Teresina. She had blushed scarlet while he was speaking, and she covered her face with both hands.

"You need not hide your face, Teresina," said Bastianello, with a little emotion. "You can show it to every one after what you have done. And so I will go on, and you must listen. Ruggiero is not a great signore like the Count of San Miniato, but he is a man. And he has two arms which are good, and two fists as hard as an ox's hoofs, and he can break horse-shoes with his hands."

"Can you do that?" asked Teresina with an admiring look.

"Since you ask me - yes, I can. But Ruggiero did it before I could, and showed me how, and no one else here can do it at all. And moreover Ruggiero is a quiet man and does not drink nor play at the lotto, and there is no harm in a game of beggar-my-neighbour for a pipe of tobacco, on a long voyage when there is no work to be done, and -"

"Yes, I know," said Teresina, interrupting him. "You are very much alike, you too. But what has this about Ruggiero to do with me, that you tell me it all?"

"Who goes slowly, goes safely, and who goes safely goes far," answered Bastianello. "Listen to me. Ruggiero has also seven hundred and sixty-three francs in the bank, and will soon have more, because he saves his money carefully, though he is not stingy. And Ruggiero, if you will have him, will work for you, and I will also work for you, and you shall have a good house, and plenty to eat and good clothes besides the gold -"

"But Bastianello mio!" cried Teresina, who had suspected what was coming, "I do not want to marry Ruggiero at all."

She clasped her hands and gazed into the sailor's eyes with a pretty look of confusion and regret.

"You do not want to marry Ruggiero!" Bastianello's expression certainly betrayed more surprise than disappointment. But he had honestly pleaded his brother's cause. "Then you do not love him," he said, as though unable to recover from his astonishment.

"But no - I do not love him at all, though he is so handsome and good."

"Madonna mia!" exclaimed Bastianello, turning sharply round and moving away a step or two. He was in great perturbation of spirit, for he loved the girl dearly, and he began to fear that he had not done his best for Ruggiero.

"But you did love him a few days ago," he said, coming back to Teresina's side.

"Indeed, I never did!" she said.

"Nor any one else?" asked Bastianello suddenly.

"Eh! I did not say that," answered the girl, blushing a little and looking down.

"Well do not tell me his name, because I should tell Ruggiero, and Ruggiero might do him an injury. It is better not to tell me."

Teresina laughed a little.

"I shall certainly not tell you who he is," she said. "You can find that out for yourself, if you take the trouble."

"It is better not. Either Ruggiero or I might hurt him, and then there would be trouble."

"You, too?"

"Yes, I too." Bastianello spoke the words rather roughly and looked fixedly into Teresina's eyes. Since she did not love Ruggiero, why should he not speak? Yet he felt as though he were not quite loyal to his brother.

Teresina's cheeks grew red and then a little pale. She twisted the cord of the Venetian blind round and round her hand, looking down at it all the time. Bastianello stood motionless before her, staring at her thick black hair.

"Well?" asked Teresina looking up and meeting his eyes and then lowering her own quickly again.

"What, Teresina?" asked Bastianello in a changed voice.

"You say you also might do that man an injury whom I love. I suppose that is because you are so fond of your brother. Is it so?"

"Yes - and also -"

"Bastianello, do you love me too?" she asked in a very low tone, blushing more deeply than before.

"Yes. I do. God knows it. I would not have said it, though. Ah, Teresina, you have made a traitor of me! I have betrayed my brother - and for what?"

"For me, Bastianello. But you have not betrayed him."

"Since you do not love him -" began the sailor in a tone of doubt.

"Not him, but another."

"And that other -"

"It is perhaps you, Bastianello," said Teresina, growing rather pale again.

"Me!" He could only utter the one word just then.

"Yes, you."

"My love!" Bastianello's arm went gently round her, and he whispered the words in her ear. She let him hold her so without resistance, and looked up into his face with happy eyes.

"Yes, your love - did you never guess it, dearest?" She was blushing still, and smiling at the same time, and her voice sounded sweet to Bastianello.

Only a sailor and a serving-maid, but both honest and both really loving. There was not much eloquence about the courtship, as there had been about San Miniato's, and there was not the fierce passion in Bastianello's breast that was eating up his brother's heart. Yet Beatrice, at least, would have changed places with Teresina if she could, and San Miniato could have held his head higher if there had ever been as much honesty in him as there was in Bastianello's every thought and action.

For Bastianello was very loyal, though he thought badly enough of his own doings, and when Beatrice called Teresina away a few minutes later, he marched down the corridor with resolute steps, meaning not to lose a moment in telling Ruggiero the whole truth, how he had honestly said the best things he could for him and had asked Teresina to marry him, and how he, Bastianello, had been betrayed into declaring his love, and had found, to his amazement, that he was loved in return.

Ruggiero was sitting alone on one of the stone pillars on the

F. Marion Crawford

little pier, gazing at the sea, or rather, at a vessel far away towards Ischia, running down the bay with every stitch of canvas set from her jibs to her royals. He looked round as Bastianello came up to him.

"Ruggiero," said the latter in a quiet tone. "If you want to kill me, you may, for I have betrayed you."

Ruggiero stared at him, to see whether he were in earnest or joking.

"Betrayed me? I do not understand what you say. How could you betray me?"

"As you shall know. Now listen. We were talking about Teresina to-day, you and I. Then I said to myself, 'I love Teresina and Ruggiero loves her, but Ruggiero is first. I will go to Teresina and ask her if she will marry him, and if she will, it is well. But if she will not, I will ask Ruggiero if I may court her for myself.' And so I did. And she will tell you the truth, and I spoke well for you. But she said she never loved you. And then, I do not know how it was, but we found out that we loved each other and we said so. And that is the truth. So you had better get a pig of iron from the ballast and knock me on the head, for I have betrayed my brother and I do not want to live any more, and I shall say nothing."

Then Ruggiero who had not laughed much for some time, felt that his mouth was twitching raider his yellow beard, and presently his great shoulders began to move, and his chest heaved, and his handsome head went back, and at last it came out, a mighty peal of Homeric laughter that echoed and rolled down the pier and rang clear and full, up to the Marchesa's terrace. And it chanced that Beatrice was there, and she looked down and saw that it was Ruggiero. Then she sighed and drew back.

But Bastianello did not understand, and when the laugh subsided at last, he said so.

"I laughed - yes. I could not help it. But you are a good brother, and very honest, and when you want to marry Teresina, you may have my savings, and I do not care to be paid back."

"But I do not understand," repeated Bastianello, in the greatest bewilderment. "You loved her so -"

"Teresina? No. I never loved Teresina, but I never knew you did, or I would not have let you believe it. It is much more I who have cheated you, Bastianello, and when you and Teresina are married I will give you half my earnings, just as I now put them in the bank."

"God be blessed!" exclaimed Bastianello, touching his cap, and staring at the same vessel that had attracted Ruggiero's attention.

"She carries royal studding-sails," observed Ruggiero. "You do not often see that in our part of the world."

"That is true," said Bastianello. "But I was not thinking of her, when I looked. And I thank you for what you say, Ruggiero, and with my heart. And that is enough, because it seems that we know each other."

"We have been in the same crew once or twice," said Ruggiero.

"It seems to me that we have," answered his brother.

Neither of the two smiled, for they meant a good deal by the simple jest.

"Tell me, Ruggiero," said Bastianello after a pause, "since you never loved Teresina, who is it?"

"No, Bastianello. That is what I cannot tell any one, not even you."

"Then I will not ask. But I think I know, now."

Going over the events of the past weeks in his mind, it had suddenly flashed upon Bastianello that his brother loved Beatrice. Then everything explained itself in an instant. Ruggiero was such a gentleman - in Bastianello's eyes, of course - it was like him to break his heart for a real lady.

"Perhaps you do know," answered Ruggiero gravely, "but if you do, then do not tell me. It is a business better not spoken of. But what one thinks, one thinks. And that is enough."

A crowd of brown-skinned boys were in the water swimming and playing, as they do all day long in summer, and dashing spray at each other. They had a shabby-looking old skiff with which they amused themselves, upsetting and righting it again in the shallow water by the beach beyond the bathing houses.

"What a boat!" laughed Bastianello. "A baby can upset her and it takes a dozen boys to right her again!"

"Whose is she?" enquired Ruggiero idly, as he filled his pipe.

"She? She belonged to Black Rag's brother, the one who was drowned last Christmas Eve, when the Leone was cut in two by the steamer in the Mouth of Procida. I suppose she belongs to Black Rag himself now. She is a crazy old craft, but if he were clever he could patch her up and paint her and take foreigners to the Cape in her on fine days."

"That is true. Tell him so. There he is. Ohe! Black Rag!"

Black Rag came down the pier to the two brothers, a middle-aged, bow-legged, leathery fellow with a ragged grey beard and a weather-beaten face.

"What do you want?" he asked, stopping before them with his hands in his pockets.

"Bastianello says that old tub there is yours, and that if you had a better head than you have you could caulk her and paint her white with a red stripe and take foreigners to the Bath of Queen Giovanna in her on fine days. Why do you not try it? Those boys are making her die an evil death."

"Bastianello always has such thoughts!" laughed the sailor. "Why does he not buy her of me and paint her himself? The paint would hold her together another six months, I daresay."

"Give her to me," said Ruggiero. "I will give you half of what I earn with her."

Black Rag looked at him and laughed, not believing that he was in earnest. But Ruggiero slowly nodded his head as though to conclude a bargain.

"I will sell her to you," said the sailor at last. "She belonged to that blessed soul, my brother, who was drowned - health to us - to-day is Saturday - and I never earned anything with her since she was mine. I will sell her cheap."

"How much? I will give you thirty francs for her."

Bastianello stared at his brother, but he made no remark while the bargain was being made, nor even when Ruggiero finally closed for fifty francs, paid the money down and proceeded to take possession of the old tub at once, to the infinite and forcibly expressed regret of the lads who had been playing with her. Then the two brothers hauled her up upon the sloping cement slip between the pier and the bathing houses, and turned her over. The boys swam away, and Black Rag departed with his money.

"What have you bought her for, Ruggiero?" asked Bastianello.

"She has copper nails," observed the other examining the bottom carefully. "She is worth fifty francs. Your thought was good. To-morrow she will be dry and we will caulk the seams, and the next day we will paint her and then we can take foreigners to the Cape in her if we have a chance and the signori do not go out. Lend a hand, Bastianello; we must haul her up behind the boats."

Bastianello said nothing and the two strong men almost carried the old tub to a convenient place for working at her.

"Do you want to do anything more to her to-night?" asked Bastianello.

"No."

"Then I will go up."

"Very well."

Ruggiero smiled as he spoke, for he knew that Bastianello was going to try and get another glimpse of Teresina. The ladies would probably go to drive and Teresina would be free until they came back.

He sat down on a boat near the one he had just bought, and surveyed his purchase. He seemed on the whole well satisfied. It was certainly good enough for the foreigners who liked to be pulled up to the cape on summer evenings. She was rather easily upset, as Ruggiero had noticed, but a couple of bags of pebbles in the right place would keep her steady enough, and she had room for three or four people in the stern sheets and for two men to pull. Not bad for fifty francs, thought Ruggiero. And San Miniato had asked about going after crabs by torchlight. This would be the very boat for the purpose, for getting about in and out of the rocks on which the crabs swarm at night. Black Rag might have earned money with her. But Black Rag was rather a worthless fellow, who drank too much wine, played too much at the public lottery and wasted his substance on trifles.

Ruggiero's purchase was much discussed that evening and all

the next day by the sailors of the Piccola Marina. Some agreed that he had done well, and some said that he had made a mistake, but Ruggiero said nothing and paid no attention to the gossips. On the next day and the day after that he was at work before dawn with Bastianello, and Black Rag was very much surprised at the trim appearance of his old boat when the brothers at last put her into the water and pulled themselves round the little harbour to see whether the seams were all tight. But he pretended to put a good face on the matter, and explained that there were more rotten planks in her than any one knew of and that only the nails below the water line were copper after all, and he predicted a short life for Number Fifty Seven, when Ruggiero renewed the old licence in the little harbour office. Ruggiero, however, cared for none of these things, but ballasted the tub properly with bags of pebbles and demonstrated to the crowd that she was no longer easy to upset, inviting any one who pleased to stand on the gunwale and try.

"But the ballast makes her heavy to pull," objected Black Rag, as he looked on.

"If you had arms like the Children of the King," retorted the Cripple, "you would not trouble yourself about a couple of hundredweight more or less. But you have not. So you had better go and play three numbers at the lottery, the day of the month, the number of the boat and any other one that you like. In that way you may still make a little money if you have luck. For you have made a bad bargain with the Children of the King, and you know it."

Black Rag was much struck by the idea and promptly went up to the town to invest his spare cash in the three numbers, taking his own age for the third. As luck would have it the two first numbers actually turned up and he won thirty francs that week, which, as he justly observed, brought the price of the boat up to eighty. For if he had not sold her he would never have played the numbers at all, and no one pretended that she was worth more than eighty francs, if as much.

Then, one morning, San Miniato found Ruggiero waiting outside his door when he came out. The sailor grew leaner and more silent every day, but San Miniato seemed to grow stouter and more talkative.

"If you would like to go after crabs this evening, Excellency," said the former, "the weather is good and they are swarming on the rocks everywhere."

"What does one do with them?" asked San Miniato. "Are they good to eat?"

"One knows that, Excellency. We put them into a kettle with milk, and they drink all the milk in the night and the next day they are good to cook."

"Can we take the ladies, Ruggiero?"

"In the sail boat, Excellency, and then, if you like, you and the Signorina can go with me in the little one with my brother, and I will pull while Bastianello and your Excellency take the crabs."

"Very well. Then get a small boat ready for to-night, Ruggiero."

"I have one of my own, Excellency."

"So much the better. If the ladies will not go, you and I can go alone."

"Yes, Excellency."

San Miniato wondered why Ruggiero was so pale.

CHAPTER XI

Again the mother and daughter were together in the cool shade of their terrace. Outside, it was very hot, for the morning breeze did not yet stir the brown linen curtains which kept out the glare of the sea, and myriads of locusts were fiddling their eternal two notes without pause or change of pitch, in every garden from Massa to Scutari point, which latter is the great bluff from which they quarry limestone for road making, and which shuts off the amphitheatre of Sorrento from the view of Castellamare to eastward. The air was dry, hot and full of life and sound, as it is in the far south in summer.

"And when do you propose to marry me?" asked Beatrice in a discontented tone.

"Dearest child," answered her mother, "you speak as though I were marrying you by force to a man whom you detest."

"That is exactly what you are doing."

The Marchesa raised her eyebrows, fanned herself lazily and smiled.

"Are we to begin the old argument every morning, my dear?" she asked. "It always ends in the same way, and you always say the same dreadful things to me. I really cannot bear it much longer. You know very well that you bound yourself, and that you were quite free to tell San Miniato that you did not care for him. A girl should know her own mind before she tells a man she loves him - just as a man should before he speaks."

"San Miniato certainly knows his own mind," retorted Beatrice viciously. "No one can accuse him of not being ready and anxious to marry me - and my fortune."

"How you talk, my angel! Of course if you had no fortune, or much less than you have, he could not think of marrying you. That is clear. I never pretended the contrary. But that does not contradict the fact that he loves you to distraction, if that is what you want."

"To distraction!" repeated Beatrice with scorn.

"Why not, dearest child? Do you think a man cannot love because he is poor?"

"That is not the question, mamma!" cried Beatrice impatiently. "You know it is not. But no woman can be deceived twice by the same comedy, and few would be deceived once. You know as well as I that it was all a play the other night, that he was trying to find words, as he was trying to find sentiments, and that when the words would not be found he thought it would be efficacious to seize my hand and kiss it. I daresay he thought I believed him - of course he did. But not for long - oh! not for long. Real love finds even fewer words, but it finds them better, and the ring of them is truer, and one remembers them longer!"

"Beatrice!" exclaimed the Marchesa. "What can you know of such things! You talk as though some man had dared to speak to you -"

"Do I?" asked the girl with sudden coldness, and a strange look came into her eyes, which her mother did not see.

"Yes, you do. And yet I know that it is impossible. Besides the whole discussion is useless and wears me out, though it seems to interest you. Of course you will marry San Miniato. When you have got past this absurd humour you will see what a good husband you have got, and you will be very happy."

"Happy! With that man!" Beatrice's lip curled.

"You will," answered her mother, taking no notice. "Happiness depends upon two things in this world, when marriage is concerned. Money and a good disposition. You have both, between you, and you will be happy."

"I never heard anything more despicable!" cried the young girl. "Money and disposition! And what becomes of the heart?"

The Marchesa smiled and fanned herself.

"Young girls without experience cannot understand these things," she said. "Wait till you are older."

"And lose what looks I have and the power to enjoy anything! And you say that you are not forcing me into this marriage! And you try to think, or to make me think, that it is all for the best, and all delightful and all easy, when you are sacrificing me and my youth and my life and my happiness to the mere idea of a better position in society - because poor papa was a sulphur merchant and bought a title which was only confirmed because he spent a million on a public charity - and every one knows it - and the Count of San Miniato comes of people who have been high and mighty gentlemen for six or seven hundred years, more or less. That is your point of view, and you know it. But if I say that my father worked hard to get what he got and deserved it, and was an honest man, and that this great personage of San Miniato is a penniless gambler, who does not know to-day where he will find pocket money for to-morrow, and has got by a trick the fortune my father got by hard work - then you will not like it. Then you will throw up your hands and cry 'Beatrice!' Then you will tell me that he loves me to distraction, and you will even try to make me think that I love him. It is all a miserable sham, mamma, a vile miserable sham! Give it up. I have said that I will marry him, since it appears that I have promised. But do not try to make me think that I am marrying him of my own free will, or he marrying me out of disinterested, pure, beautiful, upright affection!"

Having delivered herself of these particularly strong sentiments, Beatrice was silent for a while. As for the Marchesa, she was either too wise, or too lazy, to answer her daughter for the present and she slowly fanned herself, lying quite still in her long chair, her eyes half closed and her left hand hanging down beside her.

Indeed Beatrice, instead of becoming more reconciled with the situation she had accepted, was growing more impatient and unhappy every day, as she realised all that her marriage with San Miniato would mean during the rest of her natural life. She had quite changed her mind about him, and with natures like hers such sudden changes are often irrevocable. She could not now understand how she could have ever liked him, or found pleasure in his society, and when she thought of the few words she had spoken and which had decided her fate, she could not comprehend the state of mind which had led her into such a piece of folly, and she was as angry with herself as, for the time being, she was angry with all the world besides.

She saw, too, and for the first time, how lonely she was in the world, and a deep and burning longing for real love and sympathy took possession of her. She had friends, of course, as young girls have, of much her own age and not unlike her in their inexperienced ideas of life. But there was not one of them at Sorrento, nor had she met any one among the many acquaintances she had made, to whom she would care to turn. Even her own intimate associates from childhood, who were far away in Sicily, or travelling elsewhere, would not have satisfied her. They could not have understood her, their answers to her questions would have seemed foolish and worthless, and they would have tormented her with questions of their own, inopportune, importunate, tiresome. She herself did not know that what she craved was the love or the friendship of one strong, honest man.

It was strange to find out suddenly how wide was the breach which separated her from her mother, with whom she had lived so happily throughout her childhood and early youth, with whom she had agreed - or rather, who had agreed with her - on the whole almost without a discussion. It was hard to find in her now so little warmth of heart, so little power to understand, above all such a display of determination and such quiet force in argument. Very indolent women are sometimes very deceptive in regard to the will they hold in reserve, but Beatrice could not have believed that her mother could influence her as she had done. She reflected that it had surely been within the limits of the Marchesa's choice to take her daughter's side so soon as she had seen that the latter had mistaken her own feelings. She need not have agreed with San Miniato, on that fatal evening at Tragara, that the marriage was definitely settled, until she had at least exchanged a word with Beatrice herself.

The future looked black enough on that hot summer morning. The girl was to be tied for life to a man she despised and hated, to a man who did not even care for her, as she was now convinced, to a man with a past of which she knew little and of which the few incidents she had learned repelled her now, instead of attracting her. She fancied how he had spoken to those other women, much as he had spoken to her, perhaps a little more eloquently as, perhaps, he had not been thinking of their fortunes but of themselves, but still always in that high-comedy tone with the studied gesture and the cadenced intonation. She did not know whether they deserved her pity, those two whom he pretended to have loved, but she was ready to pity them, nameless as they were. The one was dead, the other, at least, had been wise enough to forget him in time.

Then she thought of what must happen after her marriage, when he had got her fortune and could take her away to the society in which he had always lived. There, of course, he would meet women by the score with whom he was and long had been on terms of social intimacy far closer than he had reached with her in the few weeks of their acquaintance.

Doubtless, he would spend such time as he could spare from gambling, in conversation with them. Doubtless, he had many thoughts and memories and associations in common with them. Doubtless, people would smile a little and pity the young countess. And Beatrice resented pity and the thought of it. She would rather pity others.

Evil thoughts crossed her young brain, and she said to herself that she might perhaps be revenged upon the world for what she was suffering, for the pain that had already come into her young life, for the wretched years she anticipated in the future, for her mother's horrible logic which had forced her into the marriage, above all for San Miniato's cleverly arranged scene by which the current of her existence had been changed. San Miniato had perhaps gone too far when he had said that Beatrice was kind. She, at least, felt that there was anything but kindness in her heart now, and she desired nothing so much as to make some one suffer something of what she felt. It was wicked, doubtless, as she admitted to herself. It was bad and wrong and cruel, but it was not heartless. A woman without heart would not have felt enough to resent having felt at all, and moreover would probably be perfectly well satisfied with the situation.

The expression of hardness deepened in the young girl's face as she sat there, silently thinking over all that was to come, and glancing from time to time at her mother's placid countenance. It was really amazing to see how much the Marchesa could bear when she was actually roused to a sense of the necessity for action. Her constitution must have been far stronger than any one supposed. She must indeed have been in considerable anxiety about the success of her plans, more than once during the past few days. Yet she was outwardly almost as unruffled and as lazy as ever.

"Dearest child," she said at last, "of course, as I have said, I cannot argue the point with you. No one could, in your present state of mind. But there is one thing which I must say, and which I am sure you will be quite ready to understand."

Beatrice said nothing, but slowly turned her head towards her mother with a look of inquiry.

"I only want to say, my angel, that whatever you may think of San Miniato, and however much you may choose to let him know what you think, it may be quite possible to act with more civility than you have used during the last few days."

"Is that all?" asked Beatrice with a hard laugh. "How nicely you turn your phrases when you lecture me, mamma! So you wish me to be civil. Very well, I will try."

"Thank you, Beatrice carissima," answered her mother with a sigh and a gentle smile. "It will make life so much easier."

Again there was a long silence, and Beatrice sat motionless in her chair, debating whether she should wait where she was until San Miniato came, as he was sure to do before long, or whether she should go to her room and write a letter to some intimate friend, which would of course never be sent, or, lastly, whether she should not take Teresina and go down to her bath in the sea before the midday breakfast. While she was still hesitating, San Miniato arrived.

There was something peculiarly irritating to her in his appearance on that morning. He was arrayed in perfectly new clothes of light gray, which fitted him admirably. He wore shoes of untanned leather which seemed to be perfectly new also, and reflected the light as though they were waxed. His stiff collar was like porcelain, the single pearl he wore in his white scarf was so perfect that it might have been false. His light hair and moustache were very smoothly brushed and combed and his face was exasperatingly sleek. There was a look of conscious security about him, of overwhelming correctness and good taste, of pride in himself and in his success, which Beatrice felt to be almost more than she could bear with equanimity. He bent gracefully over the Marchesa's hand and bowed low to the young girl, not supposing that hers would be offered to him. In this he was mistaken, however, for she gave him the ends of her fingers.

"Good morning," she said gently.

The Marchesa looked at her, for she had not expected that she would speak first and certainly not in so gentle a tone. San Miniato inquired how the two ladies had slept.

"Admirably," said Beatrice.

"Ah - as for me, dearest friend," said the Marchesa, "you know what a nervous creature I am. I never sleep."

"You look as though you had rested wonderfully well," observed Beatrice to San Miniato. "Half a century, at least!"

"Do I?" asked the Count, delighted by her manner and quite without suspicion.

"Yes. You look twenty years younger."

"About ten years old?" suggested San Miniato with a smile.

"Oh no! I did not mean that. You look about twenty, I should say."

"I am charmed," he answered, without wincing.

"It may be only those beautiful new clothes you have on," said Beatrice with a sweet smile. "Clothes make so much difference with a man."

San Miniato did not show any annoyance, but he made no direct answer and turned to the Marchesa.

"Marchesa gentilissima," he said, "you liked my last excursion, or were good enough to say that you liked it. Would you be horrified if I proposed another for this evening - but not so far, this time?"

"Absolutely horrified," answered the Marchesa. "But I suppose that if you have made up your mind you will bring those dreadful men with their chair, like two gendarmes, and they will take me away, whether I like it or not. Is that what you mean to do?"

"Of course, dearest Marchesa," he replied.

"Donna Beatrice has taught me that there is no other way of accomplishing the feat. And certainly no other way could give you so little trouble."

"What is the excursion to be, and where?" asked Beatrice pretending a sudden interest.

"Crab-hunting along the shore, with torches. It is extremely amusing, I am told."

"After horrid red things that run sidewise and are full of legs!" The Marchesa was disgusted.

"They are green when they run about, mamma," observed Beatrice. "I believe it is the cooking that makes them red. It will be delightful," she added, turning to San Miniato. "Does one walk?"

"Walk!" exclaimed the Marchesa, a new horror rising before her mental vision.

"We go in boats," said San Miniato. "In the sail boat first and then in a little one to find the crabs. I suppose, Marchesa carissima, that Donna Beatrice may come with me in the skiff, under your eye, if she is accompanied by your maid?"

"Of course, my dear San Miniato! Do you expect me to get into your little boat and hunt for reptiles? Or do you expect that Beatrice will renounce the amusement of getting wet and covered with seaweed and thoroughly unpresentable?"

"And you, Donna Beatrice? Do you still wish to come?"

"Yes. I just said so."

"But that was at least a minute ago," answered San Miniato.

"Ah - you think me very changeable? You are mistaken. I will go with you to find crabs to-night. Is that categorical? Must you consult my mother to know what I mean?"

"It will not be necessary this time," replied the Count, quite unmoved. "I think we understand each other."

"I think so," said Beatrice with a hard smile.

The Marchesa was not much pleased by the tone the conversation was taking. But if Beatrice said disagreeable things, she said them in a pleasant voice and with a moderately civil expression of face, which constituted a concession, after all, considering how she had behaved ever since the night at Tragara, scarcely vouchsafing San Miniato a glance, answering him by monosyllables and hardly ever addressing him at all.

"My dear children," said the elder lady, affecting a tone she had not assumed before, "I really hope that you mean to understand each other, and will."

"Oh yes, mamma!" assented Beatrice with alacrity. "With you to help us I am sure we shall come to a very remarkable understanding - very remarkable indeed!"

"With originality on your side, and constancy on mine, we may accomplish much," said San Miniato, very blandly.

Beatrice laughed again.

"Translate originality as original sin and constancy as the art of acting constantly!" she retorted.

"Why?" enquired San Miniato without losing his temper. He thought the question would be hard to answer.

"Why not?" asked Beatrice. "You will not deny me a little grain of original sin, will you? It will make our life so much more varied and amusing, and when I say that you act constantly - I only mean what you said of yourself, that you are constant in your actions."

"You so rarely spare me a compliment, Donna Beatrice, that you must forgive me for not having understood that one sooner. Accept my best thanks -"

"And agree to the expression of my most distinguished sentiments, as the French say at the end of a letter," said Beatrice, rising. "And now that I have complimented everybody, and been civil, and pleased everybody, and have been thanked and have taken all the original sin of the party upon my own shoulders, I will go and have a swim before breakfast. Good-bye, mamma. Good-bye, Count."

With a quick nod, she turned and left them, and went in search of Teresina, whose duty it was to accompany her to the bath. The maid was unusually cheerful, though she had not failed to notice the change in Beatrice's manner which had taken place since the day of the betrothal, and she understood it well enough, as she had told Bastianello. Moreover she pitied her young mistress sincerely and hated San Miniato with all her heart; but she was so happy herself that she could not possibly hide it.

"You are very glad that I am to be married, Teresina," said Beatrice as they went out of the house together, the maid carrying a large bag containing bathing things.

"I, Signorina? Do you ask me the real truth? I do not know whether to be glad or sorry. I pray you, Signorina, tell me which I am to be."

"Oh - glad of course!" returned Beatrice, with a bitter little laugh. "A marriage should always be a matter for rejoicing. Why should you not be glad - like every one else?"

"Like you, Signorina?" asked Teresina with a glance at the young girl's face.

"Yes: Like me." And Beatrice laughed again in the same way.

"Very well, Signorina. I will be as glad as you are. I shall find it very easy."

It was Beatrice's turn to look at her, which she did, rather suspiciously. It was clear enough that the girl had her doubts.

"Just as glad as you are, Signorina, and no more," said Teresina again, in a lower voice, as though she were speaking to herself.

Beatrice said nothing in answer. As they reached the end of the path through the garden, they saw Ruggiero and his brother sitting as usual by the porter's lodge. Both got up and came quickly forward. Bastianello took the bag from Teresina's hand, and the maid and the two sailors followed Beatrice at a little distance as she descended the inclined tunnel.

It was pleasant, a few minutes later, to lie in the cool clear water and look up at the blue sky above and listen to the many sounds that came across from the little harbour. Beatrice felt a sense of rest for the first time in several days. She loved the sea and all that belonged to it, for she had been born within sight of it and had known it since she had been a child, and she always came back to it as to an element that understood her and which she understood. She swam well and loved the easy, fluent motion she felt in the exercise, and she loved to lie on her back with arms extended and upturned face, drinking in the light breeze and the sunshine and the deep blue freshness of sky and water.

While she was bathing Bastianello and Teresina sat together

behind the bathing-house, but Ruggiero retired respectfully to a distance and busied himself with giving his little boat a final washing, mopping out the water with an old sponge, which he passed again and again over each spot, as though never satisfied with the result. He would have thought it bad manners indeed to be too near the bathing-place when Beatrice was in swimming. But he kept an eye on Teresina, whom he could see talking with his brother, and when she went into the cabin, he knew that Beatrice had finished her bath, and he found little more to do in cleaning the old tub, which indeed, to a landsman's eye, presented a decidedly smart appearance in her new coat of white paint, with a scarlet stripe. When he had finished, he sauntered up to the wooden bridge that led to the bathing cabins and sat down on the upper rail, hooking one foot behind the lower one. Bastianello, momentarily separated from Teresina, came and stood beside him.

"A couple of fenders would save the new paint on her, if we are going for crabs," he observed, thoughtfully.

Ruggiero made that peculiar side motion of the head which means assent and approval in the south.

"And we will bring our own kettle for the crabs, and get the milk from the hotel," continued the younger brother, who anticipated an extremely pleasant evening in the society of Teresina. "And I have told Saint Peter to bring the torches, because he knows where to get them good," added Bastianello who did not expect Ruggiero to say anything. "What time do we go?"

"Towards an hour and a half of the night," said Ruggiero, meaning two hours after sunset. "Then the padroni will have eaten and the rocks will be covered with crabs, and the moon will not be yet risen. It will be dark under Scutari till past midnight, and the crabs will sit still under the torch, and we can take them with our hands as we always do."

"Of course," answered Bastianello, who was familiar with the sport, "one knows that."

"And I will tell you another thing," continued Ruggiero, who seemed to warm with the subject. "You shall pull stroke and I will pull bow. In that way you will be near to Teresina and she will amuse herself the better, for you and she can take the crabs while I hold the torch."

"And the Signorina and the Count can sit together in the stern," said Bastianello, who seemed much pleased with the arrangement. "The best crabs are between Scutari and the natural arch."

"One knows that," assented Ruggiero, and relapsed into silence.

Presently the door of the cabin opened and Beatrice came out, her cheeks and eyes fresh and bright from the sea. Of course Bastianello at once ran to help Teresina wring out the wet things and make up her bundle, and Beatrice came towards Ruggiero, who took off his cap and stood bareheaded in the sun as she went by, and then walked slowly behind her, at a respectful distance. To reach the beginning of the ascent they had to make their way through the many boats hauled up beyond the slip upon the dry sand. Beatrice gathered her light skirt in her hand as she passed Ruggiero's newly painted skiff, for she was familiar enough with boats to know that the oil might still be fresh.

"It is quite dry, Excellency," he said. "The boat belongs to me."

Beatrice turned with a smile, looked at it and then at Ruggiero.

"What did I tell you the other day, Ruggiero?" she asked, still smiling. "You were to call me Signorina. Do you remember?"

"Yes, Signorina. I beg pardon."

Beatrice saw that Teresina had not yet left the cabin with her bag, and that Bastianello was loitering before the door, pretending or really trying to help her.

"Do you know what Teresina has been telling me, Ruggiero?" asked Beatrice, stopping entirely and turning towards him as they stood in the narrow way between Ruggiero's boat and the one lying next to her.

"Of Bastianello, Signorina?"

"Yes. That she wants to marry him. She told me while I was dressing. You know?"

"Yes, Signorina, and I laughed when he told me the story the other day, over there on the pier."

"I heard you laughing, Ruggiero," answered Beatrice, remembering the unpleasant impression she had received when she had looked down from the terrace. His huge mirth had come up as a sort of shock to her in the midst of her own trouble. "Why did you laugh?" she asked.

"Must I tell you, Signorina?"

"Yes."

"It was this. Bastianello had a thought. He imagined to himself that I loved Teresina - I! -"

Ruggiero broke off in the sentence and looked away. His voice shook with the deep vibration that sometimes pleased Beatrice. He paused a moment and then went on.

"I, who have quite other thoughts. And so he said with himself, 'Ruggiero loves and is afraid to speak, but I will speak for him.' But it was honest of him, Signorina, for he loved her himself. And so he asked her for me first. But she would not. And then, between one word and another, they found out that they loved. And I am very glad, for Teresina is a good girl as she showed the other day in the garden, and the little boy of the Son of the Fool saw it when she threw the gold at that man's feet -"

He stopped again, suddenly realising what he was saying. But Beatrice, quick to suspect, saw the look of pained embarrassment in his face and almost guessed the truth. She grew pale by degrees.

"What man?" she asked shortly.

Ruggiero turned his head and looked away from her, gazing out to seaward.

"What was the man's name?" she asked again with the stern intonation that anger could give her voice.

Still Ruggiero would not speak. But his white face told the truth well enough.

"On what day was it?" she enquired, as though she meant to be answered.

"It was the day when you talked with me about my name, Signorina."

"At what time?"

"It must have been between midday and one o'clock."

Beatrice remembered how on that day San Miniato had given a shallow excuse for not remaining to breakfast at that hour.

"And what was his name?" she now asked for the third time.

"Excellency - Signorina - do not ask me!" Ruggiero was not good at lying.

"It was the Conte di San Miniato, Ruggiero," said Beatrice in a low voice that trembled with anger. Her face was now almost as white as the sailor's.

Ruggiero said nothing at first, but turned his head away again.

"Per Dio!" he ejaculated after a short pause. But there was no mistaking the tone.

Beatrice turned away and with bent head began to walk towards the ascent. She could not help the gesture she made, clenching her hands once fiercely and then opening them wide again; but she thought no one could see her. Ruggiero saw, and understood.

"She is saying to herself, 'I must marry that infamous animal,'" thought Ruggiero. "But I do not think that she will marry him."

At the foot of the ascent, Beatrice turned and looked back. Teresina and Bastianello were coming quickly along the little wooden bridge, but Ruggiero was close to her.

"You have not done me a good service to-day, Ruggiero," she said, but kindly, dreading to wound him. "But it is my fault, and I should not have pressed you as I did. Do not let the thought trouble you."

"I thank you, Signorina. And it is true that this was not a good service, and I could bite out my tongue because it was not. But some Saint may give me grace to do you one more, and that shall be very good."

"Thank you, Ruggiero," said Beatrice, as the maid and the other sailor came up.

CHAPTER XII

Beatrice did not speak again as she slowly walked up the steep ascent to the hotel. Bastianello and Teresina exchanged a word now and then in a whisper and Ruggiero came last, watching the dark outline of Beatrice's graceful figure, against the bright light which shone outside at the upper end of the tunnel. Many confused thoughts oppressed him, but they were like advancing and retreating waves breaking about the central rock of his one unalterable purpose. He followed Beatrice till they reached the door of the house. Then she turned and smiled at him, and turned again and went in. Bastianello of course carried the bag upstairs for Teresina, and Ruggiero stayed below.

He was very calm and quiet throughout that day, busying himself from time to time with some detail of the preparations for the evening's excursion, but sitting for the most part alone, far out on the breakwater where the breeze was blowing and the light surf breaking just high enough to wet his face from time to time with fine spray. He had made up his mind, and he calmly thought over all that he meant to do, that it might be well done, quickly and surely, without bungling. To-morrow, he would not be sitting out there, breathing in the keen salt air and listening to the music of the surging water, which was the only harmony he had ever loved.

His was a very faithful and simple nature, and since he had loved Beatrice, it had been even further simplified. He thought only of her, he had but one object, which was to serve her, and all he did must tend to the attainment of that one result. Now, too, he had seen with his eyes and had understood in other ways that she was to be married against her will to a man she hated and despised, and who was already betraying her. He did not try to understand how it all was, but his instinct told him that she had been tricked into saying the words she had spoken to San Miniato at Tragara, and that she had never meant them. That at least was more comprehensible to him than it might have been to a man of Beatrice's own class. Her head had been turned for a moment, as Ruggiero would have said, and afterwards she had understood the truth. He had heard many stories of the kind from his companions. Women were changeable, of course. Every one knew that. And why? Because men were bad and tempted them, and moreover because they were so made. He did not love Beatrice for any moral quality she might or might not possess, he was far too human, and natural and too little educated to seek reasons for the passion that devoured him. Since he felt it, it was real. What other proof of its reality could he need? It never entered his head to ask for any, and his heart would not have beaten more strongly or less rudely for twenty reasons, on either side.

And now he was strangely happy and strangely calm as he sat there by himself. Beatrice could never love him. The mere idea was absurd beyond words. How could she love a common man like himself? But she did not love San Miniato either, and unless something were done quickly she would be forced into marrying him. Of course a mother could make her daughter marry whom she pleased. Ruggiero knew that. The only way of saving Beatrice was to make an end of San Miniato, and that was a very simple matter indeed. San Miniato would be but a poor thing in those great hands of Ruggiero's, though he was a well grown man and still young and certainly stronger than the average of fine gentlemen.

Of course it was a great sin to kill San Miniato. Murder was always a sin, and people who did murder and died unabsolved always went straight into eternal fire. But the eternal fire did not impress Ruggiero much. In the first place Beatrice would be free and quite happy on earth, and in the natural course of things would go to Heaven afterwards, since she could have no part whatever in San Miniato's destruction. Secondly, San Miniato would be with Ruggiero in the flames, and throughout all eternity Ruggiero would have the undying satisfaction of having brought him there without any one's help. That would pay for any amount of burning, in the simple and uncompromising view of the future state which he took.

So he sat on the block of stone and listened to the sea and thought it all over quietly, feeling very happy and proud, since he was to be the means of saving the woman he loved. What more could any man ask, if he could not be loved, than to give his soul and his body for such a good and just end? Perhaps Ruggiero's way of looking at the present and future state might have puzzled more than one theologian on that particular afternoon.

While Ruggiero was deciding matters of life and death in his own way, with absolute certainty of carrying out his intentions, matters were not proceeding smoothly on the Marchesa's terrace. The midday breakfast had passed off fairly well, though Beatrice had again grown silent, and the conversation was carried on by San Miniato with a little languid help from the Marchesa. The latter was apparently neither disturbed nor out of humour in consequence of the little scene which had taken place in the morning. She took a certain amount of opposition on Beatrice's part as a matter of course, and was prepared to be very long-suffering with the girl's moods, partly because it was less trouble than to do battle with her, and partly because it was really wiser. Beatrice must grow used to the idea of marriage and must be gradually accustomed to the daily companionship of San Miniato. The Marchesa, in her wisdom, was well aware that Beatrice would never see as much of him when he was her husband as she did now that they were only engaged. San Miniato would soon take up his own life of amusement by day and night, in his own fashion, and Beatrice on her side would form her own friendships and her own ties as best pleased her, subject only to occasional interference from the Count, when he chanced to be in a jealous humour, or when it happened that Beatrice was growing intimate with some lady who had once known him too well.

After breakfast, as usual, they drank coffee and smoked upon the terrace, which Beatrice was beginning to hate for its unpleasant associations. Before long, however, she disappeared, leaving her mother and San Miniato together.

The latter talked carelessly and agreeably at first, but insensibly led the conversation to the subject of money in general and at last to the question of Beatrice's marriage settlement in particular. He was very tactful and would probably have reached this desired point in the conversation in spite of the Marchesa, had she avoided it. But she was in the humour to discuss the matter and let him draw her on without opposition. She had thought it all over and had determined what she should do. San Miniato was surprised, and not altogether agreeably, by her extreme clearness of perception when they actually arrived at the main discussion.

"You are aware, San Miniato mio," she was saying, "that my poor husband was a very rich man, and you are of course familiar - you who know everything - with the laws of inheritance in our country. As our dear Beatrice is an only child, the matter would have been simple, even if he had not made a will. I should have had my widow's portion and she would have had all the rest, as she ultimately will."

"Of course, dearest Marchesa. I understood that. But it is most kind of you to tell me about the details. In Beatrice's interest - and her interests will of course be my first concern in life -"

"Of course, carissimo," said the Marchesa, interrupting him. "Can I doubt it? Should I have chosen you out of so many to be my son-in-law if I had not understood from the first all the nobility and uprightness of your fine character?"

"How good you are to me!" exclaimed San Miniato, who mistrusted the preamble, but was careful not to show it.

"Not at all, dear friend! I am never good. It is such horrible trouble to be either good or bad, as you would know if you had my nerves. But we were speaking of my poor husband's will. One half of his fortune of course he was obliged to leave to his daughter. He could dispose of the other half as he pleased. I believe it was that admirable man, the first Napoleon, who invented that just law, was it not? Yes, I was sure. My husband left the other half to me, provided I should not marry - he was a very thoughtful man! But if I did, the money was to go to Beatrice at once. If I did not, however, I was - as I really am - quite free to dispose of it as I pleased."

"How very just!" exclaimed San Miniato.

"Do you think so? Yes. But further, I wish to tell you that he set aside a sum out of what he left Beatrice, to be her dowry - just a trifle, you know, to be paid to her husband on the marriage, as is customary. But all the remainder, compared with which the dowry itself is insignificant, does not pass into her hands until she is of age, and of course remains entirely in her control."

"I understand," said San Miniato in a tone which betrayed some nervousness in spite of his best efforts to be calm, for he had assuredly not understood before.

"Of course you understand, dearest friend," answered the Marchesa. "You are so clever and you have such a good head for affairs, which I never had. I assure you I never could understand anything about money. It is all so mysterious and complicated! Give me one of your cigarettes, I am quite exhausted with talking."

"I think you do yourself injustice, dearest Marchesa," said San Miniato, offering her his open case. "You have, I think, a remarkably good understanding for business. I really envy you."

The Marchesa smiled languidly, and slowly inhaled the smoke from the cigarette as he held the match for her.

"I have no doubt you learned a great deal from the Marchese," continued San Miniato. "I must say that he displayed a keenness for his daughter's interests such as merits the sincerest admiration. Take the case, which happily has not arisen, dearest friend. Suppose that Beatrice should discover that she had married a mere fortune-hunter. The man would be entirely in your power and hers. It is admirably arranged."

"Admirably," assented the Marchesa without a smile. "It would be precisely as you say. Beyond a few hundred thousand francs which he would control as the dowry, he could touch nothing. He would be wholly dependent on his wife and his mother-in-law. You see my dear husband wished to guard against even the most improbable cases. How thankful I am that heaven has sent Beatrice such a man as you!"

"Always good! Always kind!" San Miniato bent his head a little lower than was necessary as he looked at his watch. He had something in his eyes which he preferred to hide.

Just then Beatrice's step was heard on the tiled floor of the sitting-room, and neither the Marchesa nor San Miniato thought it worth while to continue the conversation with the danger of being overheard.

So the afternoon wore on, bright and cloudless, and when the air grew cool Beatrice and her mother drove out together along the Massa road, and far up the hill towards Sant' Agata. They talked little, for it is not easy to talk in the rattling little carriages which run so fast behind the young Turkish horses, and the roads are not always good, even in summer. But San Miniato was left to his own devices and went and bathed, walking out into the water as far as he could and then standing still to enjoy the coolness. Ruggiero saw him from the breakwater and watched him with evident interest. The Count, as has been said before, could not swim a stroke, and was probably too old to learn. But he liked the sea and bathing none the less, as Ruggiero knew. He stayed outside the bathing-house fully half an hour, and then disappeared.

"It was not worth while," said Ruggiero to himself, "since you are to take another bath so soon."

Then he looked at the sun and saw that it lacked half an hour of sunset, and he went to see that all was ready for the evening. He and Bastianello launched the old tub between them, and Ruggiero ballasted her with two heavy sacks of pebbles just amidships, where they would be under his feet.

"Better shift them a little more forward," said Bastianello. "There will be three passengers, you said."

"We do not know," answered Ruggiero. "If there are three I can shift them quickly when every one is aboard."

So Bastianello said nothing more about it, and they got the kettle and the torches and stowed them away in the bows.

"You had better go home and cook supper," said Ruggiero. "I will come when it is dark, for then the others will have eaten and I will leave two to look out."

Bastianello went ashore on the pier and his brother pulled the skiff out till he was alongside of the sailboat, to which he made her fast. He busied himself with trifles until it grew dark and there was no one on the pier. Then he got into the boat again, taking a bit of strong line with him, a couple of fathoms long, or a little less. Stooping down he slipped the line under the bags of ballast and made a timber-hitch with the end, hauling it well taut. With the other end he made a bowline round the thwart on which he was sitting, and on which he must sit to pull the bow oar in the evening. He tied the knot wide enough to admit of its running freely from side to side of the boat, and he stowed the bight between the ballast and the thwart, so that it lay out of sight in the bottom. The two sacks of pebbles together weighed, perhaps, from a half to three-quarters of a hundredweight.

When all was ready he went ashore and shouted for the Cripple and the Son of the Fool, who at once appeared out of the dusk, and were put on board the sailboat by him. Then he pulled himself ashore and moored the tub to a ring in the pier. It was time for supper. Bastianello would be waiting for him, and Ruggiero went home.

As the evening shadows fell, Beatrice was seated at the piano in the sitting-room playing softly to herself such melancholy music as she could remember, which was not much. It gave her relief, however, for she could at least try and express something of what would not and could not be put into words. She was not a musician, but she played fairly well, and this evening there was something in the tones she drew from the instrument which many a musician might have envied. She threw into her touch all that she was suffering and it was a faint satisfaction to her to listen to the lament of the sad notes as she struck them and they rose and fell and died away.

The door opened and San Miniato entered. She heard his footstep and recognised it, and immediately she struck a succession of loud chords and broke into a racing waltz tune.

"You were playing something quite different, when I came to the door," he said, sitting down beside her.

"I thought you might prefer something gay," she answered without looking at him and still playing on.

San Miniato did not answer the remark, for he distrusted her and fancied she might have a retort ready. Her tongue was often sharper than he liked, though he was not sensitive on the whole.

F. Marion Crawford

"Will you sing something to me?" he asked, as she struck the last chords of the waltz.

"Oh yes," she replied with an alacrity that surprised him, "I feel rather inclined to sing. Mamma," she cried, as the Marchesa entered the room, "I am going to sing to my betrothed. Is it not touching?"

"It is very good of you," said San Miniato.

The Marchesa smiled and sank into a chair. Beatrice struck a few chords and then, looking at the Count with half closed eyes, began to sing the pathetic little song of Chiquita.

"On dit que l'on te marie
Tu sais que j'en vais mourir -"

Her voice was very sweet and true and there was real pathos in the words as she sang them. But as she went on, San Miniato noticed first that she repeated the second line, and then that she sang all the remaining melody to it, singing it over and over again with an amazing variety of expression, angrily, laughingly, ironically and sadly.

" - Tu sais que j'en vais mourir!"

She ended, with a strange burst of passion.

She rose suddenly to her feet and shut the lid down sharply upon the key-board.

"How perfectly we understand each other, do we not?" she said sweetly, a moment later, and meeting San Miniato's eyes.

"I hope we always shall," he answered quietly, pretending not to have understood.

She left him with her mother and went out upon the terrace and looked down at the black water deep below and at the lights of the yachts and the far reflections of the stars upon the smooth bay, and at the distant light on Capo Miseno. The night air soothed her a little, and when dinner was announced and the three sat down to the table at the other end of the terrace her face betrayed neither discontent nor emotion, and she joined in the conversation indifferently enough, so that San Miniato and her mother thought her more than usually agreeable.

At the appointed time the two porters appeared with the Marchesa's chair, and Teresina brought in wraps and shawls, quite useless on such a night, and the little party left the room in procession, as they had done a few days earlier when they started for Tragara. But their mood was very different to-night. Even the Marchesa forgot to complain and let herself be carried down without the least show of resistance. On the first excursion none of them had quite understood the other, and all of them except poor Ruggiero had been in the best of humours. Now they all understood one another too well, and they were silent and uneasy when together. They hardly knew why they were going, and San Miniato almost regretted having persuaded them. Doubtless the crabs were numerous along the rocky shore and they would catch hundreds of them before midnight. Doubtless also, the said crustaceans would be very good to eat on the following day. But no one seemed to look forward to the delight of the sport or of the dish afterwards, excepting Teresina and Bastianello who whispered together as they followed last. Ruggiero went in front carrying a lantern, and when they reached the pier it was he who put the party on board, made the skiff fast astern of the sailboat and jumped upon the stern, himself the last of all.

The night breeze was blowing in gusts off the shore, as it always does after a hot day in the summer, and Ruggiero took advantage of every puff of wind, while the men pulled in the intervals of calm. The starlight was very bright and the air so clear that the lights of Naples shone out distinctly, the beginning of the chain of sparks that lies like a necklace round the sea from Posilippo to Castellamare. The air was soft and dry, so that there was not the least moisture on the gunwale of the boat. Every one was silent.

Then on a sudden there was a burst of music. San Miniato had prepared it as a surprise, and the two musicians had passed unnoticed where they sat in the bows, hidden from sight by the foresail so soon as the boat was under way. Only a mandolin and a guitar, but the best players of the whole neighbourhood. It was very pretty, and the attempt to give pleasure deserved, perhaps, more credit than it received.

"It is charming, dearest friend!" was all the Marchesa vouchsafed to say, when the performers paused.

Beatrice sat stony and unmoved, and spoke no word. She said to herself that San Miniato was again attempting to prepare the scenery for a comedy, and she could have laughed to think that he should still delude himself so completely. Teresina would have clapped her hands in applause had she dared, but she did not, and contented herself with trying to see into Bastianello's eyes. She was very near him as she sat furthest forward in the stern-sheets and he pulled the starboard stroke oar, leaning forward upon the loom, as the gust filled the sails and the boat needed no pulling.

"You do not care for the mandolin, Donna Beatrice?" said San Miniato, with a sort of disappointed interrogation in his voice.

"Have I said that I do not care for it?" asked the young girl indifferently. "You take too much for granted."

Grim and silent on the stern sat Ruggiero, the tiller in his hand, his eye on the dark water to landward constantly on the look-out for the gusts that came down so quickly and which could deal treacherously with a light craft like the one he was steering. But he had no desire to upset her to-night, nor even to bring the tiller down on his master's head. There was to be no bungling about the business he had in hand, no mistakes and no wasting of lives.

The mandolin tinkled and the guitar strummed vigorously as they neared Scutari point, vast, black and forbidding in the starlight. But a gloom had settled upon the party which nothing could dispel. It was as though the shadow of coming evil had overtaken them and were sweeping along with them across the dark and silent water. There was something awful in the stillness under the enormous bluff, as Ruggiero gave the order to stop pulling and furl the sails, and he himself brought the skiff alongside by the painter, got in and kept her steady, laying his hand upon the gunwale of the larger boat. Bastianello stood up to help Beatrice and Teresina.

"Will you come, Donna Beatrice?" asked San Miniato, wishing with all his heart that he had never proposed the excursion.

It seemed absurd to refuse after coming so far and the young girl got into the skiff, taking Ruggiero's hand to steady herself. It did not tremble to-night as it had trembled a few days ago. Beatrice was glad, for she fancied that he was recovering from his insane passion for her. Then San Miniato got over, rather awkwardly as he did everything so soon as he left the land. Then Teresina jumped down, and last of all Bastianello. So they shoved off and pulled away into the deep shadow under the bluffs. There the cliff rises perpendicularly seven hundred feet out of the water, deeply indented at its base with wave-worn caves and hollows, but not affording a fast hold anywhere save on the broad ledge of the single islet of rock from which a high natural arch springs suddenly across the water to the abrupt precipice which forms the mountain's base.

Calmly, as though it were an every-day excursion, Ruggiero lighted a torch and held it out when the boat was alongside of the rocks, showing the dark green crabs that lay by dozens motionless as though paralysed by the strong red glare. And Bastianello picked them off and tossed them into the kettle at his feet, as fast as he could put out his hands to take them. Teresina tried, too, but one almost bit her tender fingers and she contented herself with looking on, while San Miniato and Beatrice silently watched the proceedings from their place in the stern.

Little by little Ruggiero made the boat follow the base of the precipice, till she was under the natural arch.

"Pardon, Excellency," he said quietly, "but the foreigners think this is a sight with the torches. If you will go ashore on the ledge, I will show it you."

The proposal seemed very natural under the circumstances, and as the operation of picking crabs off the rocks and dropping them into a caldron loses its interest when repeated many times, Beatrice immediately assented.

The larger boat was slowly following and the tinkle of the mandolin, playing waltz music, rang out through the stillness. Ruggiero brought the skiff alongside of the ledge where it was lowest.

"Get ashore, Bastianello," he said in the same quiet tone. Bastianello obeyed and stood ready to help Beatrice, who came next.

As she stepped upon the rock Ruggiero raised the torch high with one hand, so that the red light fell strong and full upon her face, and he looked keenly at her, his eyes fixing themselves strangely, as she could see, for she could not help glancing down at him as she stood still upon the ledge.

"Now Teresina," said Ruggiero, still gazing up at Beatrice.

Teresina grasped Bastianello's hand and sprang ashore, happy as a child at the touch. San Miniato was about to follow and had already risen from his seat. But with a strong turn of his hand Ruggiero made the stern of the skiff swing out across the narrow water that is twenty fathoms deep between the mountain and the islet.

"What are you doing?" asked San Miniato impatiently. "Let

me land!"

But Ruggiero pushed the boat's head off and she floated free between the rocks.

"You and I can take a bath together," said the sailor very quietly. "The water is very deep here."

San Miniato started. There was a sudden change in Ruggiero's face.

"Land me!" cried the Count in a commanding tone.

"In hell!" answered the sailor's deep voice.

At the same moment he dropped the torch, and seizing the bags of ballast that lay between his feet, hove them overboard, springing across the thwarts towards San Miniato as he let them go. The line slipped to the side as the heavy weight sank and the boat turned over just as the strong man's terrible fingers closed round his enemy's throat in the darkness. San Miniato's death cry rent the still air - there was a little splashing, and all was done.

*   *   *   *   *

So I have told my tale, such as it is, how Ruggiero of the Children of the King gave himself body and soul to free Beatrice Granmichele from a life's bondage. She wore mourning a whole year for her affianced husband, but the mourning in her heart was for the strong, brave, unreasoning man, who, utterly unloved, had given all for her sake, in this world and the next.

But when the year was over, Bastianello married Teresina, and took her to the home he had made for her by the sea - a home in which she should be happy, and in which at least there can never be want, for Beatrice has settled money on them both, and they are safe from sordid poverty, at all events.

F. Marion Crawford

The Marchesa's nerves were terribly shaken by the tragedy, but she has recovered wonderfully and still fans herself and smokes countless cigarettes through the long summer afternoon.

Of those left, Bastianello and Beatrice are the most changed - both, perhaps, for the better. The sailor is graver and sterner than before, but he still has the gentleness which was never his brother's. Beatrice has not yet learned the great lesson of love in her own heart, but she knows and will never forget what love can grow to be in another, for she has fathomed its deepest depth.

And now you will tell me that Ruggiero did wrong and was a great sinner, and a murderer, and a suicide, and old Luigione is sure that he is burning in unquenchable fire. And perhaps he is, though that is a question neither you nor I can well decide. But one thing I can say of him, and that you cannot deny. He was a man, strong, whole-hearted, willing to give all, as he gave it, without asking. And perhaps if some of us could be like Ruggiero in all but his end, we should be better than we are, and truer, and more worthy to win the love of woman and better able to keep it. And that is all I have to say. But when you stand upon the ledge by Scutari, if you ever say a prayer, say one for those two who suffered on that spot. Beatrice does sometimes, though no one knows it, and prayers like hers are heard, perhaps, and answered.

Choose from Thousands of 1stWorldLibrary Classics By

A. M. Barnard
Ada Leverson
Adolphus William Ward
Aesop
Agatha Christie
Alexander Aaronsohn
Alexander Kielland
Alexandre Dumas
Alfred Gatty
Alfred Ollivant
Alice Duer Miller
Alice Turner Curtis
Alice Dunbar
Ambrose Bierce
Amelia E. Barr
Amory H. Bradford
Andrew Lang
Andrew McFarland Davis
Andy Adams
Anna Sewell
Annie Besant
Annie Hamilton Donnell
Annie Payson Call
Annonaymous
Anton Chekhov
Arnold Bennett
Arthur Conan Doyle
Arthur M. Winfield
Arthur Ransome
Atticus
B.H. Baden-Powell
B. M. Bower
Baroness Emmuska Orczy
Baroness Orczy
Basil King
Bayard Taylor
Ben Macomber
Bertha Muzzy Bower
Bjornstjerne Bjornson
Booth Tarkington
Boyd Cable
Bram Stoker
C. Collodi
C. E. Orr
C. M. Ingleby
Carolyn Wells
Catherine Parr Traill
Charles A. Eastman
Charles Dickens

Charles Dudley Warner
Charles Farrar Browne
Charles Ives
Charles Kingsley
Charles Klein
Charles Amory Beach
Charles Hanson Towne
Charles Lathrop Pack
Charles Whibley
Charles Willing Beale
Charlotte M. Braeme
Charlotte M. Yonge
Charlotte Perkins Stetson
Clair W. Hayes
Clarence Day Jr.
Clarence E. Mulford
Clemence Housman
Confucius
Cornelis DeWitt Wilcox
Cyril Burleigh
D. H. Lawrence
Daniel Defoe
David Garnett
Dinah Craik
Don Carlos Janes
Donald Keyhoe
Dorothy Kilner
Dougan Clark
Douglas Fairbanks
E. Nesbit
E.P.Roe
E. Phillips Oppenheim
Earl Barnes
Edgar Rice Burroughs
Edith Van Dyne
Edith Wharton
Edward J. O'Biren
Edward S. Ellis
Edwin L. Arnold
Eleanor Atkins
Eliot Gregory
Elizabeth Gaskell
Elizabeth McCracken
Elizabeth Von Arnim
Ellem Key
Emerson Hough
Emilie F. Carlen
Emily Dickinson
Enid Bagnold

Enilor Macartney Lane
Erasmus W. Jones
Ernie Howard Pie
Ethel Turner
Ethel Watts Mumford
Eugenie Foa
Eugene Wood
Eustace Hale Ball
Evelyn Everett-green
Everard Cotes
F. H. Cheley
F. J. Cross
Federick Austin Ogg
Ferdinand Ossendowski
Francis Bacon
Francis Darwin
Frances Hodgson Burnett
Frances Parkinson Keyes
Frank Gee Patchin
Frank Harris
Frank Jewett Mather
Frank L. Packard
Frank V. Webster
Frederic Stewart Isham
Frederick Trevor Hill
Frederick Winslow Taylor
Friedrich Kerst
Friedrich Nietzsche
Fyodor Dostoyevsky
G.A. Henty
G.K. Chesterton
Gabrielle E. Jackson
Garrett P. Serviss
Gaston Leroux
George A. Warren
George Ade
Geroge Bernard Shaw
George Durston
George Ebers
George Eliot
George Gissing
George MacDonald
George Meredith
George Orwell
George Sylvester Viereck
George Tucker
George W. Cable
George Wharton James
Gertrude Atherton

Grace E. King
Grace Gallatin
Grant Allen
Guillermo A. Sherwell
Gulielma Zollinger
Gustav Flaubert
H. A. Cody
H. B. Irving
H.C. Bailey
H. G. Wells
H. H. Munro
H. Irving Hancock
H. Rider Haggard
H. W. C. Davis
Hamilton Wright Mabie
Hans Christian Andersen
Harold Avery
Harold McGrath
Harriet Beecher Stowe
Harry Houidini
Helent Hunt Jackson
Helen Nicolay
Hendrik Conscience
Hendy David Thoreau
Henri Barbusse
Henrik Ibsen
Henry Adams
Henry Ford
Henry Frost
Henry James
Henry Jones Ford
Henry Seton Merriman
Henry W Longfellow
Herbert A. Giles
Herbert N. Casson
Herman Hesse
Homer
Honore De Balzac
Horace Walpole
Horatio Alger Jr.
Howard Pyle
Howard R. Garis
Hugh Lofting
Hugh Walpole
Humphry Ward
Ian Maclaren
Inez Haynes Gillmore
Irving Bacheller
Israel Abrahams
Ivan Turgenev
J.G.Austin

J. Henri Fabre
J. M. Barrie
J. Macdonald Oxley
J. S. Fletcher
J. S. Knowles
J. Storer Clouston
Jack London
Jacob Abbott
James Allen
James Andrews
James Baldwin
James DeMille
James Joyce
James Lane Allen
James Lane Allen
James Oliver Curwood
James Oppenheim
James Otis
James R. Driscoll
Jane Austen
Janet Aldridge
Jens Peter Jacobsen
Jerome K. Jerome
John Burroughs
John Cournos
John F. Kennedy
John Gay
John Glasworthy
John Habberton
John Joy Bell
John Kendrick Bangs
John Milton
John Philip Sousa
Jonas Lauritz Idemil Lie
Jonathan Swift
Joseph A. Altsheler
Joseph Carey
Joseph Conrad
Joseph E. Badger Jr
Joseph Hergesheimer
Joseph Jacobs
Jules Vernes
Julian Hawthrone
Julie A Lippmann
Justin Huntly McCarthy
Kakuzo Okakura
Kenneth Grahame
Kenneth McGaffey
Kate Langley Bosher
Kate Langley Bosher
Katherine Cecil Thurston

Katherine Stokes
L. A. Abbot
L. T. Meade
L. Frank Baum
Latta Griswold
Laura Lee Hope
Laurence Housman
Lawrence Beasley
Leo Tolstoy
Leonid Andreyev
Lewis Carroll
Lewis Sperry Chafer
Lilian Bell
Lloyd Osbourne
Louis Hughes
Louis Tracy
Louisa May Alcott
Lucy Fitch Perkins
Lucy Maud Montgomery
Lydia Miller Middleton
Lyndon Orr
M. Corvus
M. H. Adams
Margaret E. Sangster
Margaret Vandercook
Margret Penrose
Maria Edgeworth
Maria Thompson Daviess
Mariano Azuela
Marion Polk Angellotti
Mark Overton
Mark Twain
Mary Austin
Mary Catherine Crowley
Mary Cole
Mary Hastings Bradley
Mary Roberts Rinehart
Mary Rowlandson
M. Wollstonecraft Shelley
Maud Lindsay
Max Beerbohm
Myra Kelly
Nathaniel Hawthrone
Nicolo Machiavelli
O. F. Walton
Oscar Wilde
Owen Johnson
P.G. Wodehouse
Paul and Mabel Thorne
Paul G. Tomlinson
Paul Severing

Percy Brebner
Peter B. Kyne
Plato
R. Derby Holmes
R. L. Stevenson
R. S. Ball
Rabindranath Tagore
Rahul Alvares
Ralph Bonehill
Ralph Henry Barbour
Ralph Victor
Ralph Waldo Emmerson
Rene Descartes
Rex Beach
Rex E. Beach
Richard Harding Davis
Richard Jefferies
Richard Le Gallienne
Robert Barr
Robert Frost
Robert Gordon Anderson
Robert L. Drake
Robert Lansing
Robert Lynd
Robert Michael Ballantyne
Robert W. Chambers
Rosa Nouchette Carey
Rudyard Kipling
Samuel B. Allison

Samuel Hopkins Adams
Sarah Bernhardt
Sarah C. Hallowell
Selma Lagerlof
Sherwood Anderson
Sigmund Freud
Standish O'Grady
Stanley Weyman
Stella Benson
Stephen Crane
Stewart Edward White
Stijn Streuvels
Swami Abhedananda
Swami Parmananda
T. S. Ackland
T. S. Arthur
The Princess Der Ling
Thomas A. Janvier
Thomas A Kempis
Thomas Anderton
Thomas Bailey Aldrich
Thomas Bulfinch
Thomas De Quincey
Thomas H. Huxley
Thomas Hardy
Thomas More
Thornton W. Burgess
U. S. Grant
Valentine Williams

Various Authors
Vaughan Kester
Victor Appleton
Virginia Woolf
Walter Camp
Walter Scott
Washington Irving
Wilbur Lawton
Wilkie Collins
Willa Cather
Willard F. Baker
William Dean Howells
William le Queux
W. Makepeace Thackeray
William W. Walter
Winston Churchill
Yei Theodora Ozaki
Yogi Ramacharaka
Young E. Allison
Zane Grey